AN AIRSHOW
TO DIE FOR

Richard Roth

FOREWORD

Set in a world of airshows, corporate jets and crop-dusting, this is a story about a young pilot who has to fly an airshow stunt that killed his brother.

It is also a story about two girls, of differing backgrounds, who are interested in him but for very different reasons.

I've flown for over thirty years and for two of them I flew on the North American airshow circuit. From that experience, I grew to appreciate the incredible skill and dedication of the pilots and performers who risk their lives to perform in front of the crowd.

Should a person wish to become an airshow pilot it is not enough to have the right plane or be able to fly gut-wrenching aerobatics. You must also be able to fly with an innate ability to know exactly where you and your plane are in a blindingly fast-moving world where one small slip can kill you.

And it will kill you in the blink of an eye.

This is a story about the people who live, fly and die in this world.

Take a seat, this book, a cup of strong coffee and strap

in. You're in for a hell of a ride!

A note: For the purpose of the story I have moved the Phoenix International airport, Sky Harbor, from its location in Phoenix to an area less built-up further west.

CHAPTER ONE

A PROLOGUE

The airshow crowd are on their feet to watch as the Stearman bi-plane blasts past them. The silence shattered as the young pilot slams the throttle forward and, engine roaring, the plane accelerates.

Craning their necks they see him climb vertically, then dive and pull out to do a four-point roll just above the runway.

They are too far away, however, to see that oil trickles from beneath the engine, backward along the belly of the plane and into the slipstream; it slowly grows in volume.

Unknowing, the pilot in the open cockpit continues to fly his show routine. He does a snap roll, a furious maneuver in a plane this big. His teeth bared as he fights the G's. Then a second roll, and a third.

Next he climbs it vertically for a hammerhead and spins down, pulling out just before hitting the ground.

The act builds to a finale and show-staff come out to the runway and pick up two long poles.

Strung out between the tall poles is a bright-colored ribbon for the 'ribbon-cut' maneuver. The pilot lines up on it, aiming for the middle.

The plane dives. The noise increases as he rams the throttle forward again, the big engine screaming.

Below, however, on the aircraft's belly, black oil streams back. It's gotten worse. A lot worse.

On the cockpit panel, the oil pressure gauge drops unnoticed into the red as the pilot concentrates on the ribbon. The plane is too far away for anyone in the crowd to see the escaping fluid.

Pointed downward the plane accelerates, the airframe shaking from the excessive speed. The noise from the big radial engine is tremendous.

The pilot rolls the Stearman upside down as he flies less than twenty feet above the ground. He's aiming to cut the ribbon with the tail.

He drops even lower. The tip of the plane's tail is just a few feet above the runway.

Faster, closer. The ground speeds by, near the young man's head in the open cockpit. The noise is overpowering as the runway reflects back the roar of the engine.

As he approaches the ribbon the pilot sees the oil. With the plane inverted it's now running down the fuselage sides in thick streams and is blown by the slipstream toward him.

His eyes narrow.

Before he can do anything the engine makes a distinct crack. Once. Twice. Then there are sickening, grinding noises as the oil-starved engine shreds metal.

A piston grinds to a halt and the connecting rod is punched out through a cylinder wall. The timing gear gets torn out of sync as the crankshaft comes apart and the engine stops producing power. The propeller now acts as an air brake.

The pilot's hand tightens on the stick. He pushes it to gain height. But there's not enough airspeed or power from the crippled engine to get the large plane away from the ground.

Inverted and shuddering, the plane slowly sinks down to the runway.

The upside-down tail touches first. Sparks fly, with a scream as metal shreds.

The tail drags on the runway, slowing the plane.

The pilot's left-hand rams the throttle back and forth, desperately trying to bring the engine back to life and pull the inverted aircraft off the ground.

But it's futile, the plane slows.

The top wing touches and the upside-down Stearman slams down, ripping open the fuel tank in the upper wing. High-octane Avgas pours out over the runway and plane.

And over the young pilot in the open cockpit.

CHAPTER TWO

IN ANTICIPATION

PRESENT DAY, SCOTTSDALE

The alarm sounds and Brooke Henderson, in her late 20's, dark-haired, both attractive and intelligent, rolls over to turn it off. She glances at the time, 5:30 am, a little earlier than she would normally set it to wake. But today was different, the G700 would be arriving before noon and she wanted to be sure everything was ready for its arrival.

Quickly going over the plans for the next few hours she knew she needed to check everything, this is going to be a big day. Brooke had worked for Executive Airways for six years and it was her belief that the company should invest in the larger plane. It was a risk, she knew that, and her career probably rested on it. But, and she smiled, she figured it a safe bet.

Gulfstream was the world's premiere corporate jet builder. Owned by billionaires, film stars and governments their aircraft were fast, luxurious and safe. Large corporate jets, they are stunningly impressive both inside and out.

She had worked hard to insure that the company bought into her concept and this particular model, the largest with the increased range. She was sure that this was the plane the company's clients would most want to use. Executive Airways had other jets, but nothing this big, with its range, or was built to this standard of luxury. This was the upgraded model, the interior had virtually every option offered by Gulfstream. She hadn't gone for the extravagant, no Hermès dinnerware or Tai Ping carpeting, her mid-west modest roots had prevailed. But this plane certainly was world-class, it could fly 12 clients from anywhere in America to most major cities around the world, non-stop in absolute luxury.

Moving from the bedroom to the bathroom she stood in front of the mirror, looking at her reflection. She looked tired and had lost some weight, too much time had been spent on the project, but she smiled, *it will be worth it.*

She quickly showered, put on makeup and dressed for the day, carefully selecting a slim-cut light gray suit, crisp white shirt and heels.

Sipping black coffee Brooke grabbed a single slice of toast and took just two bites then made for the door.

She would be picking up her boss first, he had flown in from Santa Monica, the company headquarters. But had spent the weekend with friends west of Phoenix; she had offered to collect him. It would give them, on the drive back, some time to go over the figures again for the plane.

Checking her makeup a last time in the elevator mirror, she tapped her foot impatiently on the way down to the parking level. *C'mon, c'mon. There's still a lot to do.*

Stepping out she made for her car, the company BMW parked next to the Honda hatchback she had owned since college.

She quickly sped out of the underground car park and into the early Arizona sun. She looked out at the blue sky and thought, *nothing is going to stop this, it's going to be a good day.*

CHAPTER THREE

OVER A RIVER

FOURTEEN YEARS EARLIER

The Arizona desert northwest of Phoenix stretches as far as the eye can see. The brown-grey sands and scrublands reach out for miles then meet the mountain range that dominates the horizon. A river runs from the mountains and cuts a path through valleys and the barren land. The river banks, lined with low trees, green grasses and wildflowers, show the only color in the bare scrub and desert.

In the river, a group of young boys skinny-dip; bare butts and happy faces are easily seen. They play in the red-sand shallows by the bank, the air filled with their splashing, laughter and shouts.

Till one of them screams and points. And

over their heads, just missing them by feet, a large Stearman bi-plane blasts past the boys. They scream more and wave as the plane rocks its wings back at them.

The bi-plane is painted in a beautiful deep red and has been polished multiple times so that the sunlight reflects an intense deep shine. Somebody has spent a considerable amount of time and sweat preparing this aircraft for display.

From the open front cockpit, a hand waves back to the kids on the ground. A boy of 15 sits strapped in, he half turns and looks back. "You see them?" He shouts over the roar of the large engine.

Logan Sanders in the rear cockpit, hears the young boy over his headset. "I see them."

A moment then he continues, "Take the controls, Dave. Fly for a while."

The young boy, his brother, grabs the stick with his right hand, his left goes to the large throttle lever on the cockpit wall, and his feet jam down on the rudder pedals. The plane swerves across the river as he steps on the right rudder a little too hard.

In the rear cockpit, Logan laughs but he lets

the boy get the plane back under control on his own. The plane skids from one side of the river to the other but then straightens and settles. They are still twenty feet above the water but are now flying level and straight.

Logan sits relaxed in the rear cockpit of the open biplane, he wears a headset but pushes it back off his head and it sits around his neck. He also wears a one-piece flight suit, that fits his slim frame, and a leather flying jacket with a large crop-dusters patch on the shoulder.

He checks the instruments on the aircraft panel, ensuring everything is okay. Listening to the engine he smiles, enjoying the sound of the Continental W-670, 7-cylinder radial. Its large eight-foot, two-bladed propeller busy hauling the big aircraft through the air. The abject noise of the engine, the roar, even the smell of it - the all-pervading smell of avgas and burnt oil.

Stearman bi-planes are not exactly easy planes to fly. Large and while normally docile they don't accelerate quickly, nor can they fly fast; and will take a while to recover from a mistake. The plane, at times, can take two hands on the stick plus full rudder deflections to keep it pointing in the right direction.

They will also ground-loop at the drop of a

hat when landing, from the lightest crosswind if the pilot isn't paying attention. To make it worse, the pilot sits in the rear cockpit and when taking off or landing, with the tail down, the engine and nose completely block the pilot's view. If the plane starts to ground-loop, the chances are it will finish it; coming completely around with resulting damage to wing-tips and to the pilot's pride.

But Logan loved them. Stearman BT-17s had been designed before the Second World War, thousands built and most used as trainers during the war years. This plane was one of them, he knew its history, it had spent the war years flying out of airstrips around Tucson in southern Arizona. Teaching military cadets the basics before they went on to fly advanced trainers, the AT-6 Texan, and then to fighters or bombers.

After the war years, when the trainers were no longer needed, they were disposed of. Some were burned, some scrapped and others sold off at auctions. This particular plane had been sold for a few dollars to a local dealer as surplus for no more than scrap value. Logan was certain the fuel in its tank, at the time, was worth more than the plane itself.

It was to be put to work as a crop-duster. With a large hopper tank, for chemicals, installed in the front cockpit, an air-driven pump and spray bars fitted under the wings. Working 12-hour days, 6 days a week for long summers over Arizona's corn and cotton fields.

After many years of faithful service it had been replaced by more modern crop-dusters, Piper Pawnees, planes purpose-built for spraying. Aircraft that carried more chemicals, were easily maintained and used far less fuel.

He'd worked for the company as a pilot, spraying fields, and as a mechanic when the planes needed repairs or maintenance. The owner, Wally Spence, also a pilot, first said no when Logan offered to buy the Stearman to restore and use as an airshow plane, flying aerobatics. The older man believed that both the plane and engine had been worn out years before and wasn't fit even to restore. But the young pilot was insistent, a deal was struck and Wally then also offered to help tear down and rebuild the plane with him. Starting almost immediately they set about restoring and rebuilding.

First, they tore off the fabric, the aircraft's skin, from the welded steel tube fuselage and from the wooden spar and ribs of the wings and tailplanes. What they found didn't impress them, chemicals from years of spraying had gotten into the fuselage tubing and corrosion showed on most of it.

It had taken them over a year of working weekends to complete the restoration. They had completely rebuilt the fuselage and wings, plus torn down the old engine and rebuilt that also. Adding fuel injection, to the motor, upped the power from 220 to 270hp and allowed for prolonged inverted flight.

A new propeller had been found and mounted, the old one, worn-out, filed down and cracked, was left hanging on the hangar wall. Then the aircraft was completely recovered in new fabric and dopes, and painted with multiple top coats till it shined a beautiful deep red color.

The many years of wear and tear of a hard-working crop-duster's life had done considerable damage but, looking at the final result, you would never know it. The plane was beautiful.

He was jerked out of his thoughts by a shout from Dave in the front seat as the boy waved to some fishermen sitting in an open boat.

Logan, at 31, was considerably older than his young brother, their parents for some reason had waited years before having a second child. But he'd always enjoyed his younger brother's company and took him flying whenever he could.

Dave had been about eleven when he first took him up. The boy couldn't see out of the cockpit to begin with. But, even so, he still loved to fly. Roaring with laughter when Logan would roll the plane inverted, upside down, and Dave would hang in his straps in the open cockpit, just air between him and the ground.

Their parents had died a couple of years prior in a car accident. A drunk truck driver had fallen asleep and run them off a highway, near Tempe just ten minutes from their home. The truck had rolled but its driver had barely a scratch.

Dave had been in the back of the car when it had gone off the road, he hadn't been badly hurt but had witnessed the whole event and his parent's death.

Logan shook his head, it really wasn't worth thinking about.

His brother, who at the time was 13, had taken it badly. Social services had wanted to place him in a foster home, however Logan had fought this insisting the young boy stayed with him. Although unmarried he insisted he would be more of a family for him than foster parents. Finally, the authorities agreed, and for the past two years they had shared their parent's house.

At first he would hear his younger brother cry at night, so he had the young boy move his bed in with him. Three other bedrooms stood empty as the two brothers shared a room in the otherwise big house. The boy still cried occasionally but when he did Logan would sit with him and talk quietly to reassure his young brother.

He shook his head once more, putting the thoughts out of his head, then looked out to where the river narrowed and to a large metal framework road bridge, with double arches, that crossed it.

"Hey," he shouts, over the engine noise. "You see the bridge?"

The young boy nodded.

"Let's go under," he shouts again.

His brother half-turned in his seat and he could see him smile and mouth the words, "You sure?"

The bridge was large, the span made from concrete with the big double arch metal framework above. The space below however seemed hardly bigger than a letterbox. Dark and forbidding, it looked like a coffin, not nearly big enough to get under.

"Damn right!" He shouts back, "And you fly it."

He sees the young boy shake his head.

Logan puts his hand back on the stick and waggled it gently. "I'll do it with you, feel me on the stick?"

The 15-year-old nodded, obviously more confident.

But unseen by him, Logan then removes his hand and places it back up on the cockpit coaming. The young boy effectively flying on his own.

The bridge loomed up, closer, then closer still. There looked only a couple of feet of clearance on either side of the wings; if that. The tailplane and fin would maybe clear by a few feet also. It didn't look like there was enough room for the large plane to get through.

Closer... then...

The young boy ducks, unintentionally, as the plane rockets under. But keeps the plane under control. The sound deafening as it is reflected back from the confining concrete and metal of the bridge.

Logan can hear his brother laugh as they come out from the other side. A huge grin on the young boy's face.

They fly on, still low to the river but then turn and make their way toward a built-up area. They fly between trees, and pinned to one of them is a poster advertising an airshow at Glendale County Airfield.

The Stearman flies over another road and, from an open car, some people wave to them. In the front cockpit the young boy waves back.

A few minutes later and they approach an airfield, Glendale. They look down and see taxiways and ramp areas tightly packed with Cessna's, Pipers, Beechcraft, bright-colored aerobatic aircraft, and a mass of people. It's an airshow.

CHAPTER FOUR

SKY HARBOR, INTERNATIONAL AIRPORT

14 YEARS LATER, PRESENT DAY

Still early, and with the sun only just coming up, Brooke drove the BMW west on the I-10, Maricopa Freeway, to her turn-off exit. Exiting onto South 24th then onto Old Tower Road, and through the southern entrance into the Phoenix airport.

The Sky Harbor International Airport serves America's South-West, operating from Phoenix, AZ. Covering 50 square miles the airfield is one of America's most modern and largest airfields. Purchased in 1935 the City of Phoenix bought it for $100,000. The City paid $35,300 in cash and took out a mortgage for $64,700; at the time it was considered a lot of money.

Forty-three million passengers a year flow through the airport and impressive terminal buildings, with the runways handling nearly a half million operations; landings and take-offs. PHX is one of the nation's top dozen busiest airports.

The airfield grounds cover 3,400 acres of land, and have three long runways, all running in the same direction, east to west. North Runway is designated 08/26, its compass bearings, and is the longest at 11,489 feet - over two miles long. Center Runway, 07L/25R is 10,300 feet long, a fraction under two miles. And the shortest runway is South Runway, 07R/25L at 7,800 feet, a mere one and a half miles in length.

Brooke always enjoyed driving onto the airport, her workplace since joining the company, she felt a sense of excitement as she arrived through the FBO (Fixed Base Operator) entrance; south of the terminal buildings with the traffic of airline passengers arriving and departing. The FBO area has multiple private businesses located on the airfield including two big operators, FedEx and UPS, their large freight aircraft hauling overnight and fast-delivery packages.

She passed smaller hangers that housed other aviation businesses to arrive at the impressive large purpose-built hangar that housed her company, 'Executive Airways,' a charter aircraft service; supplying corporate aircraft to businesses and individuals who need to get somewhere fast and in comfort.

Operating from multiple airports in the American South-West, the company's largest and busiest operations were based in California; but Brooke was on a mission to change that. She believed that the Phoenix operation could rival any of the other branches. Operating costs out of Phoenix were far less expensive compared to any California airport; and with this aircraft, the G700, it could be off the ground, on its way to pick up clients from their home field, and take them to London, Paris, or Beijing non-stop, within an hour. Operations would be fast, convenient and at far less cost.

She stopped the car and moved briskly into the massive hangar, she was there early to ensure everything was ready for the aircraft's arrival. This was an important day.

CHAPTER FIVE

GLENDALE AIRFIELD

FOURTEEN YEARS EARLIER, IN THE STEARMAN

Logan takes the controls from his young brother and, headset on and back to business, he brings the Stearman into the pattern; landing on the active runway.

They taxi up to the flight-line in front of the crowd. The area where performance and show aircraft prepare for their acts and routines. With a burst of power Logan spins the aircraft around and kills the engine.

Silence.

Approaching as they climb out is Wally Spence. Dave recognized him immediately, older than his brother, in his fifties, he owned the crop dusting business his brother flew for. Wally was also a pilot, but it seemed like he was always working on one of the aircraft or fixing some of the ground equipment. In fact, Dave had never seen him wear anything other than oil-stained coveralls and he always had a wrench in his hand or pocket.

He knew Wally had been married and had a daughter but his wife had left a few years earlier. His brother had told him she was convinced her husband paid more attention to aircraft than to his marriage. This was probably true, even at his young age Dave knew airplane people spent most of their time around aircraft. Probably too much time.

Wally called out, "You need fuel?"

His brother nods and an Avgas fuel truck pulls up to the plane. The driver then reels out a large hose from the vehicle, pulling it toward the Stearman. Wally steps up onto the lower wing and unscrews a large fuel cap from the tank that sits in the middle of the upper wing and over the open cockpits. Carrying 46 gallons it feeds Avgas to the engine below.

His brother then walked him to the crowd line to introduce him to the fans, people who had come to see Logan fly. He could feel his brother's hand on his shoulder.

It's obvious that Logan was popular,

shaking hands and laughing with the crowd.

However, the mood seems to change as they are approached by James Hodgeman, a Federal Aviation Administration (FAA) Inspector. In his forties, wearing a suit and tie, he contrasts the casually dressed weekend crowd.

"You're not doing that ribbon-cut stunt again are you?" Hodgeman asks. "Upside down, with your ass hanging out."

"You know what they say," replies his brother. "Give the crowd what they want."

Hodgeman stretches his neck, a characteristic he has. "What they want, is to see somebody kill themselves."

Logan doesn't answer the official, just gives a grin.

Shaking his head the FAA Inspector moves away, making for some show staff.

His brother turns back to him, "Time to make some noise." And heads for the plane. As he walks he takes off the leather jacket, "Getting warm." And tosses it back to Dave who catches it laughing.

Logan jumps up onto the wing root, climbs

into the rear cockpit and starts the engine. He waves to the crowd as he taxies away.

Dave watches as his brother heads the plane toward the runway, passing the control tower. The name GLENDALE is prominently displayed, in large letters, on the front.

As the plane taxies off, the young boy puts on the jacket, it's big for him but... and continues to watch as the plane moves away.

The plane gets to the runway, there's a roar from the engine and the Stearman accelerates down the runway and takes to the air.

CHAPTER SIX

CONVINCE ME

FOURTEEN YEARS LATER, PRESENT DAY

The BMW drives out of the International Airport, onto the I-10, heading west. The day had dawned clear, though still early in the morning it was getting hotter, the temperature had already hit 90 degrees as Brooke travels out of Phoenix.

After a half hour's drive, she turns onto a remote road. Entering a fence-lined, well-kept ranch she drives up the mile-long drive and pulls up to a large Southwest-style house to see that her boss, John Norman, was sitting waiting on the expansive porch. Dressed ready for business in a dark suit, cream shirt and tie, he stands and approaches the car as she draws up.

He enters and sits in the passenger seat. "Good morning, Brooke. Do you have the figures?"

She reaches into her laptop bag, pulls out a file, and hands it to him. Brooke also points to the cup holder, waiting for him is a freshly purchased cup of coffee; black with one sugar.

"Okay," he says, opening the pages, his tone even. "Once more. Convince me we made the right choices with this plane."

CHAPTER SEVEN

DUSTING

STILL THE PRESENT DAY

West of Phoenix the farm landscape stretches for miles with hardly a tree to be seen. Though it is still early in the year corn stands nearly six foot high; plush green and dense, large fields of the crop strike a contrast to the desert mountains that surround the plain.

Water is constantly fed from the mountains, the Colorado River, and from underground reservoirs to keep these crops green. Helped by its warm climate, Arizona is a bread basket state supplying the rest of the country with large amounts of early fresh vegetables from land claimed from the desert.

Against the farmland backdrop, the only other item to be seen this morning is a large yellow crop-duster, a Grumman G-164 Super Ag Cat, a big-engined bi-plane at work. In the air it follows a back-and-forth pattern as it flies over a field spraying the corn.

Although functional this isn't a good-looking plane, seen almost from any angle it is ugly. It's obvious the fuselage had been stretched from its original design, and its oversize squared-off tail looks like it comes from a completely different aircraft. On the nose the large Pratt & Whitney R-1340 radial engine sits too wide for the body and juts out the front and sides, again looking like it's from another plane. Each part of the aircraft seems out of proportion to the other.

But, however brute-ugly an Ag Cat seemed, however ungainly, it is tremendously good at its job. It carries a large load, over 500 gallons of pesticides in its oversized internal hopper, it is rugged and its performance is ideal for a crop-duster. It can land and take off with full loads from short dirt tracks, it is strong, can take a beating, is easily repaired if damaged, and in a crash it protects its pilot in the enclosed steel-tubed caged cockpit.

Over fields of corn this crop-duster goes, 90 mph plus, flying a mere foot or so above plant tops, spraying.

At the fence line it makes a steep turn, and the nose comes up to near vertical. It hangs, pivots around, and then back down the field for the next pass in the opposite direction.

In the cockpit a young pilot wears a headset and boom mic, jeans, a work shirt, and a baseball cap to keep a mess of dark hair out of lively eyes. He also wears an old leather flying jacket with a large crop-duster patch. This is the jacket that Logan wore, but now older and more worn. And wearing it is Logan's younger brother, Dave, it is 14 years since we last saw him; he is now 29 years of age.

At the end of the field the plane gets close to large high-voltage power lines. They loom up, but instead of turning away Dave continues spraying and flies under them. The power lines are suspended on large pylons that stand a hundred feet or so high. The cables are just high enough from the ground for a crop-duster to get under if the pilot is careful enough. At the field end, Dave turns the plane on its side and around he goes once more.

Twice more he does this, flying under the wires and around the large pylons; then the spray thins as the hopper empties. He thumbs the radio button on the control stick, *"I'm empty. On my way back."*

A voice answers him on the radio, an older

man, *"Okay, kid."*

Dave turns the duster around and heads for home. He gains a few feet for the transit back, up to about 100 feet; nothing much he's used to flying low.

He checks his instruments for the twentieth time this morning, the fuel gauge shows half full, and the head-temp, oil-temp and oil pressure are in the green, all normal. He yawns.

The plane thunders its way across the corn fields, and off to one side is a long winding road. In the distance Dave can see a car, nothing else to be seen.

He smiles, like most crop-dusters working long hours, up and down fields spraying for 12 hours straight, he gets bored and looks for ways to spice up his day.

Turning, he drops down as he catches up to the car ahead, a large, gleaming, highly polished, top-of-the-line BMW. We've seen this car before.

Getting closer, the plane's wheels skim a fence as the plane gets lower.

Closer.

INSIDE THE CAR

Brooke is still driving, and in the passenger seat is her boss. He's still going through the figures from the file and sips from his coffee.

He doesn't look up but pauses from his reading, "What time does it come in?"

"It's early, coming in at eleven."

"I'll still be in a meeting."

"Everything is arranged," she answers. "It'll be no problem. I'll meet it."

He nods and goes back to reading.

There is a roar and the car suddenly rocks as the big crop-duster buzzes them, the large plane's wheels just missing the car roof by inches. Brooke, surprised, swerves the car. She doesn't lose control, but she jumps.

John Norman spills his coffee. "Dammit!"

They see the large crop-duster as it rockets by, just above, waggling its wings at them. Neither is impressed.

IN THE AIR

Inside the duster Dave laughs as he climbs the plane back up.

Then from his radio and headset the older man's voice again, *"Dave. You still want to do your acro-ticket?"*

Dave clicks on the radio switch. *"You bet."*

And is answered, *"I'll get Sam to pull the plane out."*

An Acro-ticket: At the beginning of the airshow season, performers do a check ride, a performance evaluation, to satisfy the FAA and the International Council of Air Shows (ICAS,) that they are safe enough to perform aerobatics in front of a crowd. An examiner, a person designated by the ICAS, signs off on a card that the airshow pilot must carry while performing.

Dave turns the duster away from the road. He thinks about the car he just buzzed and laughs again, thinking. *It does get boring out here.*

To help relieve the boredom Dave also flies airshows; an aerobatic routine like his brother before him. As he passes over the field coming into land, he flies over a modern, single-wing, blue and white aerobatic aircraft, on the ground, being pushed out of a hangar.

CHAPTER EIGHT

IN THE AIR

It's later and Dave is flying the aerobatic plane. Unlike the ugly crop-duster this low-wing plane is sleek, fast and beautiful, a heart attack on wings.

Highly polished, bright blue in color with lightning stripes along the body. Its fuselage is made from welded steel tubing for strength but has a beautiful sleek outer skin made from epoxy resin fiberglass and carbon fiber. The single wing and main spar are also made from epoxy resin fiberglass with a high percentage of carbon fiber for strength. The plane is also painted in epoxy; two-pack paint for smoothness, high shine and beauty, its finish appears almost a liquid. This aircraft looks sleek and fast just standing still on the ground.

Its Lycoming AEIO-540 330 HP six-cylinder engine drives a Hartzell three-blade constant-speed prop, a big engine for a plane this size, the plane's power-to-weight ratio is exceptionally high. The acceleration of this aircraft is also breathtakingly fast. Constructed purely for aerobatics the plane is built strong, it can handle plus 16G to minus 16G, strong enough to take any stress a pilot is capable of putting on it.

Dave is sat in a semi-reclined position, designed to help handle the excessive G's that aerobatics puts on the pilot's body. Holding him in position and not allowing any movement while flying is a five-point harness. There are two straps over his shoulders, one submarine strap between his legs, and two broad straps over his waist with double buckles, To ensure he is held firmly in position there is also a ratchet that greatly tightens the harness to absolutely ensure no movement.

He rolls the aircraft over and flies inverted. Even in this position the fuel-injected engine does not miss a beat. Also, to ensure the plane can fly upside down for long periods, the oil system is designed to lubricate the engine whatever the attitude or G reading.

Dave pulls hard and hauls the plane over, eyes almost closed as the plane turns and the G's pile up. He then unloads it, stalls a wing and snap-rolls the plane, once, twice, three times.

Then dives.

Close to the ground and going fast, he turns onto his side, pulling hard as he changes direction, wingtip almost touching as he comes around. He climbs and jams on top rudder to get the plane into a knife edge, forcing the nose up then yanks off the throttle. Kicking in full rudder and down elevator he does a Lomcovák maneuver, tumbling the plane, the tail coming over the nose.

He sucks in his breath as he's hit with negative 'G's. Then full throttle again and, with excessive weight on his body as he pulls harder, it piles on positive G's and the blood drains from his head into his body. Next he bunts, quickly pushing on the stick, the plane violently pitches the nose down and the negative G's hit again; massively pushing blood from his body up to his head and brain now, the pain showing on his face.

He once explained to some friends that there's nothing like flying aerobatics, describing it as *'the world explodes in front of you.'* And continuing, *'it's like having sex and being in a car crash at the same time.'*

Yanking back the throttle he tumbles the plane again. The out-of-control maneuver sending the plane end over end.

As the plane drops he slams power back in again, the engine roars and the aircraft leaps forward picking up speed.

He steadies the plane and rolls inverted.

Going at two hundred mph and upside down, he drops lower, close to the ground. Then lower. The runway flashes by just spitting distance from his head.

ON THE GROUND

The field is home to Spence Aviation, a crop-dusting outfit. Nothing more than a landing strip, a couple of hangars, a trailer for an office and some dusters.

It looks somewhat run-down and the hangars haven't been painted for while, but the aircraft are well-serviced and the operation has an air of honest work.

Watching Dave are two people.

Samantha Spence, an attractive girl in her mid 20's, she wears jeans, a T-shirt, and a dark green flight jacket. She has long hair, tucked up into a baseball cap that she wears constantly, and an intelligent smile; no paint on her fingernails, due to her environment rather than a social statement. Sam spends her life flying dusters with the father who raised her.

Next to her stands Wally, the older man's voice from the radio and the person we first saw helping Dave's brother prepare fourteen years earlier. Now in his 60's he wears old one-piece coveralls, they are worn and weathered and so is he.

Wally holds a clipboard in an oil-stained hand, he grips it tight as he tenses up watching Dave fly. "It's too low. He's in the weeds!"

The girl answers, "You've got to be low, that's what the crowd wants."

"Don't tell me what the crowd wants, Sam. I've been flying airshows since Pontius Pilate had a license."

She grins, not intimidated by his gruff manner. "Yes, Dad."

IN THE AIR

As he rockets past, Dave looks to the side at both, then rolls upright, knife-edges and tumbles the plane once more. Then again, and again. Far too close to the runway for this out-of-control maneuver.

ON THE GROUND

Unnoticed, behind Sam and her father, a car draws up. On the door, displayed prominently, is a large government badge, FEDERAL AVIATION ADMINISTRATION. James Hodgeman wearing a suit and tie, exits and walks to both; a serious look on his face.

It's the same FAA manager from the Glendale airshow 14 years earlier, now older. He stretches his neck, the same habit as he had before.

Over the runway, Dave still flies.

Quietly, Hodgeman says, "He looks low during those tumbling maneuvres."

Both tense up and turn as he speaks. Wally answers him, "Nah, he's fine, Jim. Got to be low. That's what the crowd wants.

He looks at Sam, and gives a slight shake of the head as he realizes he just repeated what she had said a minute or so earlier.

There's no answer from the FAA official.

Wally continues, trying to lighten the

mood, "I heard you were back in the district. You got promoted?"

No answer.

Hodgeman nods to the plane, "Who is it?"

There's no reply from Wally or Sam.

The FAA official continues, "Logan's brother?"

Again, no answer for a moment, and then Wally gives a weary nod.

"He's doing his aerobatic ticket?" Questions Hodgeman.

Wally holds up his clipboard and nods again. It's pretty obvious there's a problem here.

Sam steps back, turns aside and speaks quietly into a handheld radio, *"Dave, calm it down, the FAA are here!"*

IN THE AIR

Dave clicks on the joystick radio button, *"Just having fun."* And grins. *"Tell 'em to put up the ribbon."*

ON THE GROUND

A long ribbon, the width of the runway, comes up. Suspended twenty feet above the ground on two poles held by a couple of mechanics.

Their faces are streaked with oil and they wear ill-fitting grubby coveralls. Both have big toothy grins as they look back at the FAA manager.

Sam calmly speaks into the radio again, *"Don't piss about, Dave. Just cut the damn ribbon."*

IN THE AIR

Dave dives the plane. The noise builds, he's going fast, engine at red-line. He's low, just above the ground.

Closing.

He rolls inverted. Upside down. Gets closer.

Then scant feet from the ribbon he drops even lower and goes under the tape.

Not cutting it, but flashes below it. Upside

down, 200 mph, his tail is just inches from the ground. The plane's downwash splashes gravel around on the runway.

ON THE GROUND

Samantha and Wally roll their eyes, the FAA manager shows anger and the pole-holders grin like Cheshire cats.

Hodgeman addresses Wally again, "I don't like that going-under business. He's not a damn limbo dancer. I want nothing like that in my district."

In the background, Dave rolls the plane upright and brings the aircraft around.

Coming back he dives, rolls upside down again, and cuts the ribbon cleanly with his tail.

"I'll talk to him, Jim, the kid is just..."

The FAA manager cuts him off, "Tell him, there's no special treatment. I don't care who he is, he follows the rules like everyone else."

He looks at his watch, "I need to get back." And strides off, back to his car and departs.

As they watch him leave, Sam sighs and comments, "That went well."

Minutes later Dave lands, taxies up, and stops. He spins the aircraft around in a cloud of dust and noise.

Stopping the engine and unbuckling his harness he hops out onto the wing and to the ground.

As Sam, mocking, tells him off, "That was impressive…. Not! Upside down under the ribbon. One day you'll kill yourself."

There's no reaction from him.

She continues, "So, for your funeral, did you want to be buried or cremated?"

He smiles, a slight shake of the head, "Surprise me."

She grins back, it's obvious these two get on well.

Dave turns to Wally, expecting something. But there's an empty pause.

Wally shakes his head, "You're not getting your ticket."

"What?" Dave is not sure he heard him

right.

Wally continues, "I don't know who you're trying to piss off more, the FAA or me. Out there doing 200-plus, dragging your ass on the ground."

Dave makes to answer but he's cut off by the older man. "You're too low for those tumbles. One mistake and I'm pulling bits of you out of the wreckage. Cut it out!"

He turns and walks away. And over his shoulder he also has the last word, "And get those fields finished."

Dave makes to go after him, Sam stops him, "No."

"What's wrong with him?" Upset by the older man's reaction. "He's seen me fly low below."

"I'll talk to him. Go spray."

She watches him as he angrily strides away. He gets to the crop-sprayer and steps up onto the wing, climbs up and enters the enclosed cockpit. As she turns away she hears the starter kick in and the engine fire up.

She catches up with her father but before she can say anything he stops to face her.

"He's thinking of doing the Quad-cut, isn't he?"

She doesn't answer.

Shaking his head Wally turns and continues walking, her silence has given him the answer.

"There's a million dollars, cash, for the first person who does it." She offers, following after her father. But can see the older man is not impressed.

"That's if he doesn't kill himself," Wally answers. "There's a reason it's never been done."

He stops and faces her. "And plenty of people have tried. No!" He's still angry. "He's not doing it, I'm done scraping bodies off runways."

And walks on. She follows after him.

In the background she hears the crop-duster turn onto the runway, they both turn to watch.

Brakes on, the big duster sits at the end of the strip, ready for take-off. The engine comes up in power, the big motor loud as the propeller spins faster. It churns full out, the noise deafening.

Dave, still angry, holds the plane on the brakes, the tail wheel and rear of the plane come up off the ground. The strong prop-wash over the tailplane lifts it even though the aircraft isn't moving. His feet hard down on the toe-brakes. The big plane shudders and shakes, a lot of power with nowhere to go.

Even though the brakes are locked, the plane slides forward on its stationary tires. He's losing rubber as the plane skids on, wheels not turning. Abruptly, Dave releases the brakes and the duster surges forward, quickly picking up speed, and roars down the runway on its main wheels.

He lifts a wing and the plane continues on one gear leg and wheel. He has the stick half over and some opposite rudder. It has the wing cocked in the air, a balancing act, with one wheel off the ground.

A couple of hundred feet later, the plane takes off, banking away over hedges and between trees.

Both watch as the big Ag Cat flies away, Wally shakes his head. "That boy is pushing his luck!"

CHAPTER NINE

SPRAYING, AN INCIDENT
AND A MEET

Back to the corn fields and Dave starts spraying again. The skies have darkened over, there's a storm coming. But unless or until the winds pick up or it rains hard he can continue spraying.

Starting at one corner of the field he makes his way in straight lines, guided by a light bar, in his sightline, mounted just above the engine, and linked to a GPS in the cockpit. Back and forth, he flies an even pattern across the tall high corn.

Over the north end of the field stands the high-voltage power lines on large metal-frame pylons. The main lines are made of thick cables that carry the high voltage, plus there are thinner lines on crossbars, that span above and to the side.

To continue spaying the corn he has to fly between towers and under the lines. He makes his first pass beneath them, his tail clearing them by a few feet or so. Nothing unusual here, he spends his day flying under, over or around wiring and obstacles.

The sky is much darker now, the storm is closer with lightning flashes nearby. He's not particularly concerned, just another day at the office.

Lightning strikes again, closer this time.

Trying to get into a corner of the field he goes between a couple of the towers and under the wires once more. His tail again clears the lower lines but only just.

A loud crash of thunder and lightning hits above him.

Dave sees the strike -- this is not the best place to be and turns the aircraft on its side to get away from the lines.

He's almost clear but then lightning strikes again hitting a thin line on a crossbar. For a moment nothing happens then it whips free and the line drops. Snaking out it falls on and wraps itself around the crop-duster.

Coming tight the wire tightens around the fuselage. Dave feels the jerk on the aircraft as the tethered-end snaps away from the tower, tightening it more. At the front of the plane the wire whips in tight against the spinner, slowing the propeller. This drastically reduces the power.

From the prop-spinner the wire trails over the wing and is wrapped around the body of the plane. From the rear, the line snakes back from the tailplane, hard up against the rudder and jamming it.

Just seconds and he's in real trouble.

With reduced power, it's hard to stay in the air plus with the rudder jamming it's hard to turn. Pushing hard with his left hand on the throttle Dave tries to increase the engine rpm, the jammed spinner still slows the propeller and nothing changes. He fights the controls to keep the plane flying.

Below him are the fields of six-foot corn, with nowhere to put down.

IN THE PLANE

He jams down on the radio switch, and talks into the headset mic, some urgency in his voice, *"Wally, gimme the frequency for Phoenix International."*

It only takes a moment then he hears the older man over his headset, *"What's wrong?"*

Dave replies, *"Got a wire wrapped around me."*

"Damn! Hold on."

A moment then Wally replies again, *"Don't go to the International."*

Dave snaps back, *"Just give me the frequency!"*

Wally replies, *"It's 118.7, don't go there, go to Glendale."*

Dave ignores him and retunes his radio. Quickly dialing in the frequency.

Phoenix airport is a couple of miles ahead of Dave, and he's making his way there, but slowly dropping the whole time. The plane is not making consistent enough power to stay in the air.

He can see the airport fence and further on, standing tall, the control tower. First, however, he has to get the aircraft across a small lake, he's just a few feet above the water. To stop the aircraft from stalling he drops the nose and the plane slowly comes down. His wheels touch and bounce on the water's surface.

Skipping across the water like a kid's flat stone. Spray kicks up each time his wheels touch but he's staying in the air. Just.

He heads for the low, rocky shoreline. Reaching the water's edge he can't get it higher and the right gear leg and wheel smack into rocks.

It kicks the plane back into the air but rips off a wheel. Which goes bouncing along the ground till it smashes into tall corn.

He looks down, straining against his harness to see under the wing. He has a right-gear leg, but no wheel -- this is getting worse.

Dave shakes his head, *another shit day at the office.*

Now he's over fields again, below him stands tall corn, unworkable for a landing with or without landing gear.

He checks the radio, ensuring he's got the right frequency. And jams down on the joystick radio button, *"Phoenix Tower, this is Seven Whiskey Mike, got a problem. From the west, heading your way."*

AT THE TOWER

At the air traffic control tower at Phoenix International a controller looks up from his display as he hears the radio message and answers, *"Say aircraft type and problem?"*

He also catches the eye of Hodgeman, the FAA manager in his normal place of work. He moves to stand next to the controller, who flips on a speaker so the manager can hear.

Both of them grab binoculars and look outside to the west.

The reply comes over the speaker. *"A crop-duster. I got a wire wrapped around me."*

The controller relaxes, it's not a 747 or anything of great importance. He looks up at Hodgeman who, straight-faced, gently shakes his head.

Over his headset, the controller replies, *"You'll have to land somewhere else. We're maxed out here."*

"No. Coming there."

The controller looks outside at the busy airport. Twenty or so passenger aircraft are lined up for take-off on two of the runways, the third taken up by a line of jets in the sky in the process of landing. Plus a stream of aircraft are taxiing towards and from the runways.

This is a busy place, he replies, *"No can do. All runways are loaded. Go to Glendale, you're right by it."*

From the speaker they hear a single word. *"No!"* And the sound of a radio being switched off.

IN THE AIR

Barely staying in the air Dave makes the busy airport. He manages to hop over the fence. There are large aircraft everywhere.

He's just a few feet above the ground, heading straight for a group of passenger jets on the taxiway.

Toward a stationary Boeing 737 next in line for take-off -- it's going to be hard to miss it.

At the last second he pulls up and just manages to get over, his one remaining wheel bumps it just above the cockpit.

INSIDE THE BOEING

At the controls, the Boeing pilots are head-down doing their checklists; startled they both look up and at one another at the bump above their heads.

ON THE TAXI-WAY

The crop-duster comes down on the taxiway.

Landing on the one wheel, weaving, it's going the wrong way into a line of taxying passengers jets.

Running on one tire, going fast enough to keep the other gear-leg in the air. A wing cocked in the air, the same balancing act Dave did when he took off. But this time not for fun.

On one wheel he goes under the wing of an Airbus, then under the body of an even larger 747.

Dave can see the pilots and passengers as they look out wide-eyed as he passes under their aircraft.

Other large passenger jets have to get out of his way, they're pulling off the taxiway onto the grass, he is causing chaos.

BY A LARGE HANGAR

At the aircraft ramp and taking delivery of a new, large, stunningly beautiful Gulfstream 700 corporate jet is Brooke Henderson. This is the plane she has been waiting for.

Standing on a small podium with a lectern, she is in the middle of making a speech to a group of employees regarding the new plane, and does not see the crop-duster coming their way. "... we, at Executive Airways," she says. "Are very happy to take delivery of this new, beautiful Gulfstream jet. It will become, and deservedly so, the flagship of our fleet..."

Standing by her is a uniformed delivery pilot, he has just flown in the G700. He does see the crippled crop-duster doing its balancing act coming their way. It looks like it's heading toward an open area, but...

His eyes narrow, he doesn't think it's a

factor, but he calmly puts a pen into Brooke's hand as she's speaking. He places the delivery papers on the lectern and guides her into signing them as the crop-duster gets closer.

Still in mid-speech, Brooke continues, "This is, without a doubt, the most luxurious executive aircraft on the market. By this time tomorrow it will be taking its first corporate flight with..."

She hasn't noticed the delivery pilot is guiding her into signing.

BACK AT THE PLANE

At first it looks like Dave's aircraft is going to miss the jet, but an eighteen-seat twin-Otter aircraft, 'GRAND CANYON SIGHT-SEEING TOURS' painted on the side, taxies out in front of him.

In the large panoramic windows, families can be seen. Dave sees kids staring wide-eyed at him. "Shit!"

He rams the control stick hard over to the right, slamming down the wing and wheel-less leg.

Still going fast the gear-leg digs in and the

plane slews to the right, skidding away from the twin-Otter, sparks flying, toward the executive jet.

The dragging lower wing slides under the nose and into the large Gulfstream's nose gear. The gear collapses and the jet slowly goes nose down and rests with its tail obscenely high in the air.

Dust settles around the damaged duster, now mated with the badly flawed corporate jet.

Silence.

Brooke, stunned, looks at the duster and crippled aircraft, then to the factory-delivery pilot. "You see what he's done to your plane?"

"No. Not my plane. Your plane." He quickly stuffs the freshly signed delivery papers into his pocket giving her the bottom copy and a Gulfstream logo key ring. "Your receipt, keys."

"What?" But then ignores him as, with paperwork and keys in her hand, she goes after Dave.

Stood by the crop-duster's wing and

furious she calls out to him, still in the plane. "You... look what you've done. It's new, it cost $75 million."

Un-strapping, Dave struggles to get out of the Ag-Cat, the small cockpit door falls off its hinges.

She moves closer to the nose of the crippled jet. "Look at it." Opened mouth, she can't believe it. "What did you think you...?" Words fail her.

Dave steps down from the wing onto the ground, shaking his head, trying to clear it. Looking at the two crippled planes, he silently curses under his breath, "Damn."

He is approached by the delivery pilot. "You're Dave Sanders, right, you fly airshows?"

Dave looks up. Nods.

The delivery pilot continues, "Yes. Seen you fly."

From behind them, Brooke has overheard, and continues softly, "An airshow pilot." Shakes her head.

It's obvious the delivery pilot is impressed though, and tells her, "One of only a dozen who can do the ribbon cut stunt."

Unimpressed, her voice is quiet, "A stunt pilot." Then with feeling, directly to him, "You jerk. Another hot shot. I should have known."

Dave reacts, "What!"

She answers, "I've had a lifetime of pilots. Heads stuck up their rear-ends. No wonder you can't see where you're going."

He's starting to take offense. "Hey, that's not—"

However she continues, "So, tell me, what are you going to do about this?"

He's getting angry. "Well, under normal circumstances, we could have dinner, discuss this and—"

"And what? With your pilot charm and good looks, maybe I'll forget about it?"

She shakes her head again, turns on her heel and walks away to inspect the damage.

A car arrives and out jumps the FAA district manager, Hodgeman, angry but under control. He makes for Dave. "Was that you? Busting into closed airspace, going under taxying planes, bumping a jet, scattering aircraft. And this...?"

For a moment words fail him. But

continues, "This will cost you your ticket."

The delivery pilot has been looking over Dave's plane. "It's not his fault." He turns back to them. "Got a wire wrapped around his plane."

Hodgeman takes a moment to look over the crop-duster. Still shaking his head, he's not convinced.

The pilot adds, "And, if he hadn't swerved he would have hit the sightseeing plane." He points at the departing aircraft.

The FAA manager steps away, pauses, thinking about it, then returns and gets in Dave's face. Quiet but determined. "I don't care about your brother or what happened in the past... I'm not going through this again. Anything else and your ticket's gone."

He strides off, gets into his car, and departs.

There's a silence and Dave turns to Brooke. "How about that dinner? We could discuss how —"

She answers, "Screw you!"

"That would be good too."

"Not in your lifetime." And she turns on her heel to walk away. But stops, a pause, then turns back, stands in front of him and calmly continues. "You know, what we have here is a failure to communicate."

She smiles, looking at him for acknowledgement.

He smiles back.

She then slaps his face, hard. Very hard. "Now we're communicating!"

Dave steps back -- that hurt.

She adds, "I'll expect you in my office tomorrow morning at nine. By then we'll have an idea how much this will cost and how you'll pay for it." And she strides off.

The delivery pilot steps next to Dave. "Yep, no question," he says, as they watch her leave. "I think she likes you."

And walks away laughing.

CHAPTER TEN

A DISAGREEMENT

THE NEXT DAY

A Jeep enters the International Airport General Aviation section, the area used by civil aviation organizations, the Fixed Base Operator, FedEx, UPS, air freight, and corporate jets. It drives into the carpark for the Executive Airways building and parks. Dave exits and enters the building.

He takes the elevator to the third floor and strides into a well-appointed office and reception area. There is leather seating, solid wood fixtures and expensive carpeting; some money has been spent here. Standing to one side two uniformed corporate pilots chat, relaxed.

On a door, behind a secretary's desk, a small sign states 'Brooke Henderson, Vice-President,

Corporate Travel.'

Dave speaks to the receptionist at the desk, "I have an appointment with Ms Henderson at nine."

She looks up at the clock on the wall, which shows 9:25, and answers, "I'll let her know you're here."

Dave sits and picks up a magazine as the pilots turn to him. The first asks, "Dave Sanders, right? Seen you do your act."

The other pilot continues, "We're thinking of doing a routine."

Dave answers, "Do it. I'll fly with you."

The elevator doors open and out strides John Norman, the president of Executive Airways. He was in the car earlier with Brooke Henderson.

Both corporate pilots straighten up and respectfully greet him. He nods, not paying attention to them.

He asks the receptionist, "Ms Henderson in?"

"She is, Mr Norman, I'll let her know you're here."

He turns and notices Dave, their eyes meet and hold for a moment, it's obvious he knows who Dave is. Neither acknowledges the other.

Norman holds the gaze for a moment then turns back and makes for the office. He enters. It is a modern, tasteful, corner office, clean and uncluttered. With two large windows, one overlooking the International Airport and corporate aircraft parked immediately in front of the building.

Brooke is smartly dressed in a skirt, blouse and heels, her jacket hangs on the back of her chair. She sees him and starts to get up. He motions her to sit.

Norman asks, "Okay, Brooke. How much?"

"Six hundred thousand, give or take."

"How much is the deductible?"

"We pay the first half million."

Shaking his head, "That figures. What about their insurance? The dusting company?"

"Won't pay." She sighs, frustrated. "He was instructed to land at Glendale, flew right by it. A quiet airfield, he should have landed there."

"Does he have anything? Or is this going to be our loss?"

"He owns a Jeep and half an aerobatic aircraft he built with a friend. Worth eighty-thousand, tops. The spraying season's coming to an end, he then lives by flying airshows. They're dangerous and pay virtually nothing."

"So he has nothing, earns nothing, and could be dead by this time next month?"

She nods, as he thinks about it.

After a moment he continues, "This is what we'll do, either he pays or he works it off here. He'll fly our small stuff or swing a wrench. And no airshows."

Her forehead creases. "You sure this is how you want to handle it? It will take a long time to..."

He's determined. "I'm not letting some flying bug-sprayer damage my plane and walk away. One way or another, he pays."

Norman waits for an answer but gets none.

"Make it happen, Brooke, I want that money."

He exits her office.

Brooke swings her chair and looks out the window at the busy airport. Shakes her head then speaks into the intercom, "Send him in, please."

A minute and Dave enters. "I take it that was your boss. People out there wet themselves just watching him walk by."

"We have a problem, Mr Sanders. The aircraft you damaged is going to cost a half million plus to repair."

"Call me Dave."

"Mr Sanders, how are you going to pay?"

"A few dollars a week."

"This is serious, either you pay or—"

Dave changes his tone, more serious, "I'll sell what I have, and make payments till it's paid off."

"That'll take a lifetime. This is what you'll do."

Dave waits.

"No more spraying, Mr Sanders. You'll work

for us. Flying our small planes and we always need mechanics."

He's not happy, but he's considering it.

"There's a condition. No more airshows. You're no good to us dead."

This has an effect on him. "I'm not giving up airshows."

She continues, "This is a step up. You'll get medical benefits, uniform, a pension."

She can see he's not impressed.

He answers, "Pension? A uniform?"

"Yes, we'll—"

"And no airshows." He's getting ready to leave. "No thanks."

"This has got to be better than—"

"I'm not a flying chauffeur." He interrupts her, getting angry, and he heads for the door.

"Don't you walk out on me."

He's not stopping and she's becoming upset. "Mr Sanders, there's no choice."

He pauses, makes to say something, but changes his mind. And leaves, slamming the door.

A moment passes and the receptionist enters to check on Brooke. "You okay?"

Brooke stands, moves to the corner window and looks down on the carpark. Still bristling. She watches as, below, Dave exits the building.

Without looking back from the window, she says, "You know, there's a set of very simple rules for dealing with pilots."

"Rules?" The receptionist isn't sure how to answer.

"Yes," Brooke continues. "Unfortunately, nobody knows what they are."

The receptionist is still not sure what to say.

"Damn him!" Brooke grabs her jacket and makes for the door.

CHAPTER ELEVEN

LET'S FLY

In his Jeep, Dave drives back to the airfield. Behind him, a top-of-the-line BMW catches up.

On the wrong side of the road, driving fast, Brooke draws level. She opens the passenger window and shouts to him over the wind noise, "We need to talk. Pull over."

He cups his ear and makes like he can't hear her, shrugs his shoulders and continues driving. But coming fast from the opposite direction is a truck. The driver blasts his horn.

Brooke sees it at the last moment and has to drive onto the opposite shoulder to avoid it. She slides to a stop, not hurt, but shaken. Angry, she hits the steering wheel with both hands.

Dave watches her in his rear-view mirror, he may have a problem with this girl but he's concerned; he continues driving.

Ten minutes later he arrives at the crop-duster airfield, parks outside a hangar and walks in.

It's a working hangar for the spraying operation and looks like it. Tools, work benches, shelving with aircraft parts, an arc welder in the corner, nitrogen bottles, plus a propeller and an old wing hanging on the wall -- this place could do with a clean-up.

By the open doors stands a yellow Stearman. The same kind of older biplane Dave's brother flew at airshows, but this one is set up for spraying. Old and beat up but looks like it still has some life in it. It has a hopper, for the chemicals, in the fuselage behind the engine and spray bars under the wings

Working on it, Wally closes an engine cowling.

Dave asks, " You finished this?"

"Yep, done." He replies. "I'm going to test-fly it."

"I'll do it." Dave continues. He hears a car draw up outside. "I need to blow off some steam. It's fueled up?"

Wally nods.

The young pilot sees Brooke as she enters. In her smart business clothing and heels, she's a complete contrast to the surroundings.

He turns back to the plane, starts a pre-flight inspection, takes off the pitot tube cover, checks the prop for nicks or cracks, and ignores her.

She follows him as he walks around the plane. "Mr Sanders, we need to talk."

Dave doesn't answer, he continues checking the Stearman biplane, examines the tires and brakes then steps up onto the lower wing to check the fuel in the upper.

She's getting angry. "I'd appreciate it if you'd stopped ignoring me."

From the side, Wally watches, amused.

Dave hops down from the wing, still in the middle of the pre-flight but answers her, "Ms Henderson, I don't have time to stop and chat. I have to work, got some bills I need to take care of."

He goes to the rear and checks the tailplane and elevators. "You know how it is. Rent, utilities, and a $75 million jet to pay for."

Then inspects the rudder. "Nothing much, but I need to get in some overtime to cover it all."

"We need to discuss this."

"And I need to fly." He's not stopping his walk-round and, at the front now, he pulls through a half dozen prop blades to clear any oil.

"I'm here to talk about this rationally," she continues.

But he's still not paying attention.

Brooke stops following him and stands with her hands on her hips. She's angry but her voice is even. "You know, I have seen you fly. You have a habit of buzzing cars. Forget the offer of flying for us. I have a better job, one more suited to your talents. It involves a broom and the floor of our hangar."

Dave bristles but controls his temper. "I have to go."

Wally joins him and helps push the plane out of the hangar.

She knows she will lose him in a minute. "I'm coming with you."

Still pushing the plane, he answers, "You do

not want to fly with me."

Brooke takes a look at the Stearman. It's obvious from her face she's never been close to a plane like this. "You're right, I don't, but..."

Determined, she pulls herself up onto the lower wing of the beast, her high heels and business suit not helping. Taking off her shoes, she drops them in the rear cockpit. Pulls her skirt higher and struggles her way in. It takes her a moment to get over the coaming and into the small cockpit.

From the ground, Dave looks up trying not to smile. "Ms Henderson..."

She looks down at him. "Yes?"

"The passenger sits in the front."

"What?"

"The controls..."

Standing, determined, she looks at the other cockpit. It's empty and bare, other than the seat and harness, it is obviously for the passenger. Then looks down at hers, it has the only controls and instruments. She's in the wrong place.

She shakes her head. "I knew that."

Then pulls herself out of the rear and maneuvers her way into the front, her skirt riding high on attractive legs. Dave and Wally try not to look.

He jumps up onto the lower wing root, easily swings his leg over the rear sill, enters, and sits. Then stands up again, and reaches down as he picks up a pair of high heels.

Holds them up. "Yours?"

Brooke turns and snatches them from him. "Thank you."

He's trying hard not to grin. But gets back to business and switches on the electrics, and primes the engine. Then hits the starter button.

Just as she speaks, "We'll begin with a payment plan that..."

Her words are lost as the engine bursts into power. The propeller spins into a blur.

Dave releases the brakes and taxies the plane away from the hangar and onto the runway. As he comes to a stop Brooke tries to start the conversation again. But he pushes the throttle forward, connects his harness and starts the pre-flight run-ups to test the mags and carburetor heat.

The propeller churns at 1800rpm, and the noise of the radial engine is considerable. Then, with checks complete, and leaving the power set from the run-ups he releases the brakes and starts down the runway. Then pushes the throttle all the way forward for full power, with a roar the plane accelerates, and the tail comes up quickly.

As they leave the ground Dave pulls the plane onto its side and cranks around the hangar.

IN THE AIR

Brooke slides sideways in her seat, she does not have her seatbelt and shoulder straps on. Dave gestures for her to face forward and put on her harness.

She turns, in time to see tall trees as they fly between them, and under the lower branches. Her eyes widen, looking up at them. Brooke grabs for the harness, fumbles as she connects it, but manages and pulls tight on the straps.

Dave grins as he starts, "Would passengers return to their seats..." He's been waiting a long time to be able to do this old routine.

They fly close to the ground, the lower wing brushing a bush as they turn.

He's laughing now. "... and raise their seat-backs to the upright position."

The Stearman wing-tip just misses ducks in a small pond.

Her hair swirls in the wind as he climbs the plane, she half-turns and tries to continue, "Don't think this stops me from telling you..."

Dave holds his hand to his ear, the look on his face, *'what was that?'*

She tries once more, "I said, this won't..." But he isn't paying attention. He dives the plane to gain speed and, close to the ground, pulls the aircraft up and into a loop.

The Stearman climbs, then pulls upside down and over, coming down the backside like an express train.

Her hands, white-knuckled, grip the cockpit sides.

Out of the loop and close to the ground he rolls the aircraft over and flies the plane inverted as she hangs, helpless, in her straps. Upside down, her face angry, she mouths the words,

"Dave Sanders you are a..."

The rest is lost in the noise.

BACK ON THE GROUND

Wally's daughter Sam joins her father and both watch the plane. It climbs, then with its nose in the air, rolls over and spins down. One turn after another.

She asks her father, "What's he doing?"

"Flight-test. Has the Executive Airways girl with him."

In the background the plane still spins, dropping lower.

Sam's not pleased. "Why?"

IN THE AIR

Dave continues his routine, "On behalf of your captain and crew of crop-duster airways, we hope you've had a pleasant flight and that you'll fly with us again."

Brooke sits white-faced and angry as the world spins around her.

A couple of minutes later and Dave brings the plane back to the airfield. He comes over the fence, lands, and quickly taxies up to Wally and Sam.

Power and mixture are pulled back and the engine stops. Mags and electrics off, and Dave hops out ignoring the girl. He speaks to Wally, "The plane's fine, no problems."

Back in the front cockpit, Brooke, angry, fumbles with the seat buckle. Her hand shakes as she tries to release the harness. Sam, who can see that Brooke is having trouble, jumps up on the wing to help her.

Brooke, trembling but finally free of the harness, gets out of the cockpit and steps down onto the ground. She walks unsteadily after Dave who makes his way to the hangar.

She's furious. "Don't think it ends here. You'll pay for our plane."

Wearing one shoe, the other in her hand, she turns and makes her way to the car. Trying to straighten her clothes and hair.

Wally catches up with Dave. He walks with

him. "That's a hell of a way to treat a girl you like."

"I don't like her," answers the young man.

"Right. You keep telling yourself that."

They stop and stand together to watch as she slowly drives away, the car weaving from side to side.

After a moment Wally continues, "So, how much do you have to pay them?"

CHAPTER TWELVE

HOW MUCH?

BACK IN THE CROP-DUSTER HANGAR

It's later the same day, Dave and Sam approach the damaged Ag-Cat crop-duster, the plane that Dave smashed into the executive jet. It's up on jacks at the back of the hangar.

"How much?" She's not sure she heard right. "Half a million? Crap!"

He shrugs. "That's what they want - to replace the nose gear, it's not a hard repair, but damn, that's an expensive plane."

She shakes her head. "How are you going to pay it?"

No answer from Dave. He's checking the damage to the Ag-Cat. Crawls underneath it and calls out to Sam, "Left wings are fine. Fuselage, engine, and prop okay, not touched. Most of the damage is to the lower right wing and main gear."

She's thinking about what he said. "You could try working for them. Pay off the bill over time and live a normal life. You won't be doing airshows, but you'll be flying. Hauling passengers isn't all bad."

Dave looks up.

She continues, "Trouble is, once people have flown with you, most never want to fly again."

She gets a thin smile from Dave.

Still underneath, he goes back to inspecting the plane, pulling aside the fabric on the lower damaged wing; exposing busted ribs and cracked spar. "Got to rebuild this wing."

"Here," she says. "Wally made out your ticket."

He puts out his hand and she passes him the small signed card. She goes on, "You'll do the show this weekend?"

Dave nods.

She gives it a thought, then, "Don't do the Quad-cut."

CHAPTER THIRTEEN

AT FALCON

Falcon Field airport lies in Mesa County, to the northwest of Phoenix. Originally owned by the US government it got its start as an airfield for Southwest Airways in 1940. Then, within a year, it became a training field for British pilots in the Second World War.

These young recruit pilots traveled a long way from their home, first by ship to Canada then by train to Arizona. For them, a complete change in weather from damp, gloomy Britain to the heat and endless sunshine of Mesa and the desert South-West.

Falcon Field, at the time, covered 500 acres of land, surrounded by mostly empty farmland. The training airfield consisted of two large Quonset hangars, a control tower and two runways. Plus the offices, mess halls, sleeping quarters, and the officers' club were in a square-shaped campus south of the tower.

Nearly three thousand British pilots were trained at Falcon or, as it was officially known at the time, the Fourth British Flight Training School Stateside, or No. 4 BFTS. After training they returned home to fly Spitfires, Lancasters and numerous other RAF aircraft.

After the war, the airfield was deemed as surplus to requirements and sold to the City of Mesa for $1, with the condition it remained an airport. The city modernized it and upgraded the field for general aviation use.

Today the officers' club is gone, as is the original control tower, however, somewhat modernized, the two Quonset hangars remain. Two runways also still serve the airport, side by side the longest is 5,100 feet.

Set back from the runways is the modern control tower with 'FALCON FIELD' in large letters displayed prominently on the front.

Normally a bustling general aviation

airport, today it hosts an airshow. Set back from the runways on the tarmac it is packed with people and aircraft. The noise of powerful engines, show announcers, music, and the buzz of a large crowd all add to the excitement of the day.

Dave and Samantha walk through the large crowd of people. Sam stops at a vendor stand and orders an ice cream from a young man.

As he serves her, he remarks, "I've seen you guys before." He motions over at Dave, "He's doing an aerobatic act here, today, right?"

She nods.

He looks at her flight jacket and asks with a smile. "Are you a pilot?" It's obvious he's flirting.

"Yeah. But don't tell my dad." She smiles back, looking over her shoulder. "He thinks I'm a lap dancer."

He laughs, he's interested in her. But she turns and joins Dave.

They continue walking through the crowd till they arrive at the aerobatic plane, cordoned off with the other show planes. The aircraft looks beautiful. Even standing still the low-wing plane looks sleek and fast, the strong sunlight reflects off the highly polished paint.

"Time to make some noise." Dave ducks under the cordon, climbs up and stands on top of the wing.

Raising an arm, he waves to the crowd which applauds him back. A young gladiator, in a one-piece flight suit and leather flying jacket, going out to do battle with lions.

AT THE CROWD-LINE

Brooke Henderson, dressed casually in slacks and a light shirt, moves through the people.

BACK AT THE AIRCRAFT

Now in the cockpit, Dave starts the engine. It snarls into life, bellowing noise from the large exhaust. He snaps on the harness, adjusts his headset, and taxis away from the flight-line.

In the background the announcer tells the crowd about Dave Sanders, an up-and-coming young airshow performer.

Samantha moves back to stand in front of the crowd. She sees Brooke, she's not pleased but can't ignore her. Beckons her under the tape.

They stand together as Dave roars down the runway.

Brooke is the first to speak, "I was in the neighborhood."

Sam answers her, "Sure." But doesn't believe her.

An awkward pause between them. But then broken by Brooke, "I checked up on his plane. You own half of it?"

"Dave and I built it, with some help from my dad, a couple of years back," replies Sam. "Took a while."

"You also do aerobatics?"

"My dad taught me, almost from the first day he took me up. Said it was part of learning to fly. I love it."

IN THE AIR

As his wheels come off the tarmac, Dave

turns on his airshow smoke. From a holding tank, mineral oil with paraffin added is injected directly into the hot engine exhaust where it burns. The smoke pours out, leaving a thick white trail behind him.

Within feet of the ground he snap-rolls the plane, the wings coming dangerously close to the runway during the violent maneuver. He does another snap-roll the other way. Then he rolls the plane level, just for a brief moment, and from there he aileron-rolls it again and again. Not stopping, one after another, just feet from the runway.

The wingtips almost touch the ground as he spins around each time. The crowd roars approval, people get to their feet, and heads crane to see more.

At the runway end, Dave turns and climbs his aircraft inverted to a thousand feet, back to show-center and hangs vertically on the propeller before dropping tail first. The plane slides backwards then cartwheels to the side, once, twice. And dives.

His plane screams down, pulling out just feet before hitting the ground. It barrels along the runway in front of the excited crowd.

ON THE GROUND

The two girls continue to watch.

"One mistake," remarks Brooke. "A slip…"

And Sam completes the sentence for her, "… and he's in the dirt."

Sam looks at the other girl, Brooke's eyes never leave Dave's aircraft as it roars along the crowd line just feet from the runway.

"Does he always fly this low?" Asks Brooke.

There's no answer from Sam.

Brooke continues, "I didn't think they didn't let you fly this close to the ground?"

"We're allowed below 500 feet when crop-dusting or over an airfield."

"That's it?" Asks Brooke.

Sam shrugs.

IN THE AIR

On the cockpit panel the altimeter rises and dips as Dave flies his routine. The G meter needle slams between positive 8 and negative 6, and the airspeed indicator shows over 200 mph. Plane and pilot under great stress.

Coming out of a dive he loops the plane again, recovering only feet from the ground. Engine screaming as the plane barrels along.

It's obvious that there's some kind of problem here, each time Dave gets close to the ground he's playing a game of chicken with himself. Closer and closer each time.

IN THE PLANE

The strain shows on his face, as the G's pull down, his teeth clenched. Grunting, tensioning his body muscles to stop the blood from draining from his brain. To hold back the grey as his brain tries to black out.

One gloved hand clenched around the stick, the other pulls up the sleeve of his jacket.

BACK ON THE GROUND

Brooke asks, "He always wears that jacket?"

"Won't fly without it." Answers Sam.

Brooke queries Sam with a look but the other girl doesn't elaborate.

As they watch, Dave blasts out of a maneuver and again a wingtip almost brushes the ground. If this isn't a death wish it's pretty convincing.

The crowd roars, on their feet again surging forward, screaming, as if they smell blood.

Brooke goes to leave. "I can't watch this."

Sam has little patience with her but knows that Dave pushes it when he flies. "It's coming to an end."

In the air, Dave gets away from the ground and slows it down.

He completes a last maneuver then, amidst applause, comes in and lands.

"You like him don't you?" Sam remarks.

She gets a shake of the head as an answer.

The look on Sam's face is -- sure.

Brooke continues, "This is business. I don't need more trouble in my life right now."

AT THE PLANE

On the ground now, Dave taxies back to the flight-line. Stops, opens the canopy, and climbs out. He stands on top of the aircraft wing and raises both arms to face an approving, applauding crowd. They push forward but are held back by security people at the tape line.

Jumping down from the wing, Dave moves to them to sign autograph books. Surrounded by kids, teenagers and adults, pushing and jostling.

Brooke turns to the other girl. "They want…?"

Sam answers, "If a performer kills himself, they'll have his autograph."

The other girl is not sure what to say as Sam continues, "The trick is not to kill yourself."

BACK AT THE PLANE

Dave sees Brooke standing with Sam, he continues to sign but looks up at her between people.

She looks away.

He goes back to signing autographs, still swamped with people. Brooke turns back to watch him as he handles the crowd, watching his face as he answers questions from a couple of teenage girls; both of whom are more interested in him than an autograph. He is good-looking, she thought, but damn he is arrogant.

Another thought comes into her head, something about if things had been different and … but she quickly stops. *He's not her type, she didn't need more problems. Pilots are too full of themselves. What was that saying? The difference between pilots and God is that God doesn't think he's a pilot.*

No, she definitely didn't need another pilot in her life.

He moves to join them; the teenage girls still trail him, till he joins Brooke and Sam, then both turn away obviously disappointed.

He smiles at Sam then speaks to Brooke, "I didn't expect to see you here."

"Just here to keep an eye on our investment. You owe my company a lot of money."

He finishes signing the last couple of autographs. Gives back pens and autograph books, and turns back to her. "I'll do the Quad-cut."

"The airshow stunt?"

Dave nods. Brooke sees Sam react badly to this but she doesn't say anything.

She continues, "It's not just the money is it?"

The question hangs. He doesn't answer and it's easy to see that Samantha is not happy about this.

He changes the subject, "I'm sorry about the other day. Flying you like that."

She thinks this over, something on her mind. Then answers him, "I've got my car, I'll drive you back, and we can talk."

He nods, "Okay." Then to Sam, "Take the plane home, will you?"

Easy to see by Sam's face she's not happy, but answers, "Sure. Samantha Spence, aircraft valet and ferry service. Did you want it polished? Vacuumed? Detailed?" But she gets no answer from him. "No? -- Then I'm out of here."

Sam climbs up onto the wing and drops into the cockpit as they leave. She starts the engine, angrily revving up the engine, the prop-blast kicking up dirt.

Then calms herself and taxies away.

CHAPTER FOURTEEN

A SUNDAY DRIVE

Brooke and Dave walk amongst the parked cars at Falcon Field, away from the crowds. Row after row, thousands of vehicles, in tightly packed lines.

They look up at a beautifully polished vintage plane as it circles the field for the crowd. Making small talk.

He points, "A DC3, great old plane. They've been used for everything, even executive planes a long time ago."

"Not one we would use today," she says. "Maybe we can get you to have a look around ours. See if we can change your mind about us."

They arrive at her upmarket BMW.

Dave remarks, "Nice car. Yours?"

She smiles, "It belongs to the company. I

have it to pick up important clients."

They get in. It's a beautiful car inside, top-of-the-line, full leather, a Bose system, the works.

Buckling up, she notices that Dave doesn't. "You don't wear a seat belt?"

"Not in cars." He looks around. "Looks fast... Why don't you let me drive, take you for a ride you might enjoy?"

She answers, "Could be more than you can handle."

"Could be exciting."

She starts the car. "The insurance company doesn't like excitement," she answers. "They would say you should take this slowly... carefully."

Brooke turns to look behind her and... In reverse, she floors it!

The car leaps back. Brooke spins the wheel quickly and speeds off down the lane of cars in reverse.

Fast. Very fast!

At the intersection she doesn't slow down but pulls on the handbrake, one-handed she spins the wheel again and skids the front end around the turn.

Then again she boots the accelerator. And down the rows of cars they go, fast, still going backwards.

Dave, uncomfortable, is not sure about this.

Brooke drives, looking back, her face calm. Foot hard down on the accelerator, the RPM's on redline.

Passing row upon row of cars. Backwards. The lane widens and she has enough room to turn. Just.

Only just!

She pulls on the hand brake and again spins the wheel one-handed. Without slowing the car does a 'J' turn and changes ends.

The car doesn't slow, just changes direction. It's still at speed but now going forward. Engine screaming. She redlines it at each gear change.

People hurriedly get out of the way as Brooke speeds along the car rows. Approaching the exit she pulls on the handbrake again, and the car goes into a fast sideways skid.

And the car slides sideways out onto the main road, sliding sideways through a cap between cars.

Almost unnoticed Dave puts on his seatbelt. Out of the corner of her eye Brooke just catches it and remarks, "Wise decision," with a laugh.

Accelerating, they go from zero to illegal in three seconds flat. Brooke overtakes other cars as if they were standing still

Speeding down the road, the BMW weaves in and out of heavy traffic, traveling at twice the speed of others. It's obvious she's handled a car like this before.

INSIDE THE CAR

Hanging onto the strap, Dave's face is pale. "Where'd you learn to drive like this, Daytona?"

"Nope." She replies, "Toughest training course in the world, worked my way through college delivering Domino's pizzas."

Into the city they go, people walking and crossing the road have to hurry out of the way. Brooke travels dangerously close to a little old lady, about to cross, who jumps back at the last moment. And shakes a furled umbrella at them. "I'm walking here!"

Back inside the car Brooke calmly continues her on-the-edge driving. Coolly, professionally, but fast, now heading out of town.

Under ten minutes and they arrive at the crop-duster airfield, with Dave still pale and hanging onto his strap. She slows to sixty miles an hour, and they slide sideways through the airfield entrance.

Approaching the hangar, it looks like Brooke is not going to stop. At the last moment she pulls on the handbrake, the back of the car comes around and she slides sideways into a parking spot.

And parks...

... perfectly!

Watching are Wally and Sam, who has just landed, both grinning.

Dave, white-faced, slowly gets out. As he exits, Brooke leans over and smiles brightly. "Enjoyed our chat, Mr Sanders. We must do it again."

And speeds away, a cloud of dust, and out of the airfield.

A moment passes and Dave wobbles past Wally and Sam. He looks to them both. "Not a word. Don't say a word."

A laughing Sam follows the still-pale Dave into the hangar. "So, who took who for a ride?"

Before he can answer, Wally appears at the door. "Tomorrow, you're spraying up near Parker. Both of you. Be here early."

CHAPTER FIFTEEN

PAWNEES FLY

It's early the next day at the hangar, the sun just coming up. The mechanics and Wally pull out two, single-wing, Piper Pawnee crop-dusters and prepare them for the day's work. Helping them are Dave and Sam.

Sam loved the Pawnees, her father had bought these 15 years earlier when she had been small.

When she stood by them, at the time, she had appeared tiny. The Pawnees towered over her. Not particularly large planes, but to her they had appeared awesomely big.

The PA-25 Piper Pawnee was one of the first dedicated crop dusting planes. It had been designed in the late 1950s early 60s, they were well respected but it was joked that they were made from spare parts from Piper's other aircraft; high-wing Super-Cubs and Tri-Pacers in particular.

Certainly, the wings were from the Cub but instead of mounting them high on the fuselage, above the pilot's head, they were now mounted as a low wing on the larger body of the Pawnee. The tail-plane, fin, and rudder were taken straight from the PA-22 Tri-Pacer, the main gear was standard issue Piper, and various other pieces came from other Piper models.

The pilot's cockpit sits high on a downward-sloping forward fuselage to give the flyer an exceptional view when flying close to the ground, spraying and landing. These pair were later versions, D models, with fuel tanks in the wings, instead of one large tank just behind the engine, and came with a choice of two big Lycoming motors, 235 or 260hp. Wally opted for the bigger engine, to help deal with Arizona's hot and harsh flying conditions.

Rugged as hell, Pawnees were immediately accepted as a work-horse plane in the growing crop-dusting world. The first models could carry 145 gallons of pesticides, were simple to maintain, easy to repair, and could operate from small strips, roads, or rough tracks. Pilots also liked them as the enclosed cockpit came with a welded steel tube protective cage that surrounded and protected them in a crash. A serrated wire cutter ran up the centre of the windshield with a line that stretched from the cockpit top back to the top of the tail. All designed to stop a wire or cable, if hit, from cutting off a pilot's head or taking off the tail.

With its fuselage built from welded steel tubing, and its wings made with aluminum ribs mounted on extruded aluminum spars, it was covered in fabric; except for around the engine compartment and hopper. And was exceptionally robust; though the doped fabric skin could easily be punctured or cut. However, it could, within an hour or so, be repaired. A fabric repair could be done where the aircraft stood, in a hangar or just as easily outdoors by the side of a landing strip.

Bend or damage the steel tubing and the repair would take a little longer, but it was known for farmers or crop-duster operators to do it themselves; cutting out and welding busted-up steel tubing, and the Pawnee could be flying again within an hour or so.

Their flying characteristics were straightforward, the Pawnee handled like a well-manned but somewhat bigger, heavier Super-

Cub; it was a forgiving tail-dragger with no inherent bad habits. When landing in strong cross or tail winds the plane, like all tail-draggers, could easily ground-loop, but if the pilot stayed ahead of the aircraft and worked the rudder then the plane would stay pointed in the right direction. However, if a pilot was heavy-footed and landed with his feet high on the rudder/brake pedals and, unintentionally, pushed on the powerful brakes, he could easily stand the Pawnee up on its nose. So pilots learned to land with their feet low on the rudder pedals and constantly work the rudder, keeping the plane straight.

Sam loved flying them, it felt like this was her plane. She had grown up learning to fly in her father's 65hp Piper J-3 Cub, the Pawnee to her was a large version of that plane; albeit somewhat heavier, a lot heavier actually, over double the weight and size, and with a much bigger engine. But, it felt like an extension of herself, this large hard-working plane with its somewhat heavy, but honest, flying characteristics.

Sitting in the high cockpit she could get it into the smallest, roughest strips and then out again with a full load. And if the winds were blowing a gale, her feet would be dancing on the rudder pedals keeping the beast straight and pointing in the right direction. She'd never ground-looped one, or put one up on its nose, and did not intend to do so.

She especially remembered her first flight in one. Pawnees only came with one seat so her first flight in one was flown on her own. Most planes come with at least two seats and dual controls so you would go up with an instructor who would teach you how the plane flies. And after several flights, take-offs and landings, and when your instructor thought you were competent, you would then be sent off alone. But with a Pawnee, with its one seat, and no second chances, your first flight in it would be solo... she would be on her own.

She had learned in the J-3 as a young teen, her father teaching her from the moment her feet could reach the rudder pedals and she could see out of the cockpit. Solo-ing it on her sixteenth birthday, she had taken her Private Pilot flight test in it at seventeen. Her father had then taken her flying in and had her check out in a two-seat Super Cub, a slightly bigger version of the J-3 and, soon after, he had her fly the Pawnee.

She remembered that first day in the much larger crop-duster, just getting into it was different. The J-3 and the Super Cub were both small high-wing aircraft, you opened the door and just stepped into the cockpit, not that much different to getting into a car. Not so the Pawnee, she remembered climbing up on the back of the low wing, taking two more steps up, then turning and facing back toward the tail of the plane. Instead of a door, the Pawnee comes with a large window you climb through; getting in it's easier to face backwards, swing one leg over the sill then swing your other leg in while turning, pivoting, and sit down facing forwards.

She had climbed in and sat for twenty minutes or so getting herself used to the high-mounted cockpit and the view out over the forward-sloping nose. Her father explained to her the differences in handling between the J-3 Cub with its tiny, hand-start, 65hp engine and this beast with its 260hp power plant.

She still remembered him explaining to her, "Sam, this plane is big but without a load it has a lot more power than it needs. For take-off you don't need to use it all; feed in the throttle slowly." He continued, "It'll accelerate fast, really fast. There's a lot of torque so push in right rudder, more than you'd expect, or the tail will come round and you'll ground loop it."

He then went on to describe its landing characteristics and gave advice for the first, and critical landing. "Don't try and three-point it on, you'll get the sight picture wrong and mess it."

He continued and pointed out the sloping nose and while it gave great visibility when the pilot was used to it, for first landings it gave a different view than a normal tail-dragger. Virtually all other taildraggers had noses that didn't slope and consequently, if you try to land with the regular sight picture, holding the nose high in the air for a three-point landing, the plane will stall and drop. The resulting bounce on the shock-cords sprung landing gear will start a PIO; Pilot Induced Oscillations. All you can do is slam in the power, take off and fly around again.

"Don't try and land the first couple of goes," he went on. "Just fly down the runway, with a little power, a couple of feet up. Do it a couple of times. Then fly it again like you're not going to land, but slowly reduce the power, don't try and hold off. Half flaps and come in like you're doing a wheel landing. Fly just above the runway, reducing power and the plane will land itself.

Keep it straight with the rudder and you'll be home free."

Butterflies in her stomach, she psyched herself up for the takeoff. Both fuel pumps and mags on, trimmed slight nose-up and mixture full rich, she slowly but firmly pushed forward the big throttle. Immediately the big Pawnee accelerated, she added in right rudder to keep the nose pointing in the right direction, then she pushed the stick forward gently and the tail came up. More right rudder needed now. And within seconds she felt the plane wanting to fly, the aircraft light on its main gear, she eased back on the stick and was off the ground. Just like that! *WOW, the J-3 or Super-Cub never felt like that!*

It climbed like a maniac, she could hold the nose high and it just kept climbing. She flew for twenty minutes or so, doing some general handling. Did a couple of stalls at 60 mph or so, then a couple of slips. Steep turns left and right then a wing-over. Enjoying the power this plane had. Then, she thought, it's time to land this bad boy.

She turned back to the airfield and prepared herself. She did a big student-type approach, remembering the old saying that a good landing starts with a good pattern. She flew the 'downwind' at 900 feet, reduced power to about 800 rpm, 80 mph, mixture full-rich, half flaps, fuel pumps on, no need for carb heat - this is Arizona. Then turned onto the 'base leg', still half flaps, remembering what her father had said, then onto 'final' at 300 feet and lined up on the runway.

A couple of practice runs, carrying a little power and flying just above the runway. Then it was time to do it for real. Her first landing was near perfect, she flew just above the runway and gently reduced power and all three wheels touched down as if on their own. With a big grin on her face, 17-year-old Sam slowed the plane in front of her dad and Dave. And, after getting thumbs up from them both, she took off again, doing a wide pattern to bring the plane back again. Once more she flew down the runway with just a little power. Then, reducing the throttle, it touched down again perfectly on three wheels, her grin even bigger.

Putting power in she took off and once more around she went. Maybe a bit too confident this time, she went to repeat her previous successes but something went wrong. A small bounce to begin with but then the bounces got worse with the plane rearing up between touch-downs; oscillations, the heavy sprung landing gear kicking her back into the air each time. Quickly slamming in full throttle, she held the stick gently back and the plane roared back into the air.

Going around again and this time she did exactly as her father said, fly it down the runway with a little power, don't try to make it land, nor try to hold it off, just ease back on the throttle, keep it straight, and it will land itself. And, to the Pawnee's credit, it did just that.

Taxing quickly back to where her father and Dave stood she got out to applause from both of them.

"That's it, we're done working for the day, you need a beer. Let's go to the bar," said her dad.

She laughed, "I'm not old enough, I'm sure the bar management might have something to say about it."

"Screw 'em," stated her father. "You just turned 17, you weigh hardly 100 pounds and you just solo-ed a tail-dragging, big-engined, hairy-assed Pawnee. They'll give you a beer."

All three laughed and thirty minutes later

she, her father and Dave sat in the local bar and each had a cold, frosty beer in front of them.

Yes, she thought, I will always remember my first solo flight and landing in a Pawnee.

Still smiling to herself she finished the pre-flight inspection of her Pawnee and looked over to see Dave as he completed his. Wally and the mechanics finished mixing the chemicals and loaded each aircraft.

Then Dave and her climbed into the cockpits and ran through the pre-flight checklists, started their engines and taxied to the runway.

They took off together as a pair, both aircraft side by side, one slightly behind the other.

During their working day they stayed together, coming and going for fresh loads in formation.

As they did each field, spraying, they stayed as close as possible, wings almost touching and again, one wing slightly behind the other.

Two working planes, worn, functional, painted yellow and stained with the chemicals of their trade. A pair of ugly ducklings.

But here they're in their element, flying, they're beautiful.

The day progresses till it's late afternoon.

Dave and Sam turn to go home for the last time and begin to play. First, a dog-fight, one on the other's tail, mock-fighting, having fun.

Two young people wearing jeans, T-shirts, flying jackets, dark glasses, tight gloves, aviation headsets, and boom-mics; they are flying and they are alive.

They loop their planes, one on the other's tail. Then do barrel rolls, one after another, an aerial game of tag.

The dog-fight gives way to an exciting fast-tempo dance. Dave leading, Sam just behind. She flies as aggressive as he. She gets on his tail, chasing him, her prop almost chewing into his rudder.

They fly over saddles and down hillsides through rocky terrain, just feet from the ground.

Between trees, along roads, down ravines, dropping lower and lower.

Down to the river, side by side, both planes skip their wheels gently on the surface; once, twice. Wing tips skim the water as they turn, then up sheer cliff faces.

The dance slows.

With their engine noise in the background, almost quiet, it is surreal, an aerial ballet dance in the setting blood-red sun.

But then the mood changes. They fly near a double-arched bridge, and Dave, who has seen it, his face set as memories flood back, abruptly turns away from the structure. He moves further over the river and he bumps his wheels on the surface. Not gently, but hard this time. Then harder, bouncing the wheels on the surface, jarring the aircraft. The water is like concrete at this speed.

He bumps his wheels once more, pounds on the surface and the plane rears up. Then again.

IN SAM'S COCKPIT

Sam sees the plane kicking up from the

contact with the water's surface. She thumbs her mic, "Dave. You okay?"

IN THE AIR

No reply.

The road from the bridge turns and runs alongside the river, and Dave moves over it. Bangs his wheels again, this time on the tarmac. Again. Pounding.

IN SAM'S COCKPIT

Sam jams down on the joystick mic switch. "Cut it out. You'll kill yourself."

It's like he doesn't hear her. He pounds the wheels down once more on the road surface. Jarring, rearing up almost out of control.

Blinded by the setting sun, he doesn't see a large semi-truck on the road till the last moment. Its horn blaring, coming towards him, looming up.

He pulls up, and almost misses it, but bumps the cab top with his wheels. The aircraft skidding away.

The truck swerves almost broadside across the road.

It snakes wildly past a large sign, 'ARIZONA WELCOMES CAREFUL DRIVERS.'

Brakes squealing the driver gets it under control and screams up at the departing crop-duster, "Asshole!"

BACK IN THE AIR

The two planes climb up, Sam brings her plane in close to him. Flying side by side.

She looks across at the other Pawnee, trying to make eye contact with him. Calls him over the radio, "Dave."

No answer.

She raises her voice, shouting over her headset, "DAVE!"

Finally, he looks over.

She calls him again, "You finished?"

For a moment there's nothing, then Dave nods and she sees him relax.

Over his headset, he hears her, "Let's go home."

The tension gone, side by side, they fly back to the crop-duster field.

CHAPTER SIXTEEN

PLANE WASH

The two aircraft return, hopping over the boundary fence, and land. Both taxi up to the hangars, and with a roar from the engines they pivot around and park up.

Closing down the dusters Dave and Sam jump out.

Wally is waiting for them. "Dave, the girl from Executive Airways phoned, she's coming over."

Dave asks, "Now?"

Wally nods, then to Sam, "You hungry? Wanna go eat?"

"I'll stay and help put the planes away."

Wally replies, "No. We're eating. Been a long day."

He turns to Dave. "Wash the planes off. Put

'em to bed."

Dave nods, as Sam and her father make their way to her dad's truck.

About to get into the vehicle Sam stops and looks back, *she'd rather stay.*

But hears her father, "Come on, get in. Let them talk."

Taking off his jacket, Dave gets a hose, bucket, and soft broom. He starts by putting water through the plane's hopper, and through the side loader. Then out through the pump, valves, spray bars, and nozzles, washing out chemical residue. Then moves the hose to the outside, washing chemical stains and work-a-day dirt from the first plane.

As Wally's truck leaves the field, Brooke's BMW arrives. Driving normally, she parks. Exiting the car she comes and joins him.

The atmosphere between them is a little cool.

She is the first to speak. "I came to apologize, I shouldn't have driven you like that."

He smiles, "I deserved it."

For a moment neither speaks, there's an awkward silence between them.

Dave breaks the ice. "We got off to a bad start. I'd like to start over."

A pause but then she nods her agreement. Then asks, "Need a hand with this?"

"You ever wash planes, it's pretty simple?" He asks.

"As a kid I spent time on a farm," she says. "This can't be much different to washing down tractors."

He gives her the hose and they start on the first Pawnee, Dave scrubs with the soft broom while she sprays.

"After we finish these," she says. "Come take a look at our planes. See how we do things."

It's still awkward between them but he agrees.

They continue washing the Pawnees but then she accidentally catches him with the spray. "Sorry."

He shakes his head - no worries.

A minute later and he's sprayed again. Another accident? She smiles an apology.

He's not convinced. Retaliates by flicking water at her with the broom. But misses.

A minute later and he walks out from behind the plane to be caught once more by Brooke's spray. Moving quickly he tries to scoot away.

Moments later and again he's sprayed. He's had enough and decides to lay a trap. Waits till she appears around the tail and throws the entire contents of the bucket.

And misses completely. She retaliates by soaking him this time. It becomes a one-sided battle with Brooke winning, laughing, and chasing him around the plane with the hose.

He's also laughing, trying to get away but she's persistent and eventually he's wet through. In his jeans and his soaked shirt sticking tight to his body, he looks like a finalist in an all-male wet T-shirt contest.

It's a little awkward between them.

Dave is the first to speak. "There's a dry shirt in my Jeep."

"I'll get it for you."

She returns as he removes his wet shirt. His tanned body gleams in the lights. Brooke holds out the fresh shirt, he reaches for it and their hands touch. They are close and there's a moment between them.

The mood is broken as a large corporate jet flies low overhead.

"That's our plane," she says. "Repairs are done, it's finishing its post-repair flight test."

He takes the dry T-shirt.

"Let's go back," she continues. "I'll show you around our operation."

"Brooke...". He steps closer.

She kooks at him, waiting.

They're close, she holds his gaze - yes?

He says, "I'll drive this time."

Laughing they head for his Jeep.

CHAPTER SEVENTEEN

IN THE COCKPIT

It's getting dark as Dave and Brooke arrive at the closed-up Executive Airways hangar. They park and exit his Jeep.

The hangar side door opens and two of the company pilots step out. The same two that talked to Dave in Brooke's office area. They address Brooke.

"It flies as good as new," the first pilot says.

"Any problems?" She asks.

The pilot shakes his head. "We'll have a report on your desk first thing."

The second pilot turns to Dave. "We've been practicing our act, we'll be competition to you soon."

Dave smiles.

Brooke says goodnight to the pilots as they leave. Then to Dave, "Let's do the five-cent tour."

They enter the large hangar, it's a complete contrast to Dave's crop-duster world. Pristine clean, air-conditioned, the walls are spotless white, with a highly polished floor, a flight-planning room and well-furnished offices stretch along one side. A fitting place for expensive corporate aircraft.

They walk between a couple of smaller jets and reach the pride of the fleet, the stunningly beautiful Gulfstream 700.

A large world-class corporate aircraft, capable of carrying 12 to 20 people in opulent splendor. The largest and considered, perhaps, the most luxurious of business jets. Fitted with Rolls-Royce engines, giving it a range of 7,500 miles, and capable of cruising at a height of 51,000 feet; miles above most commercial passenger jets.

"You ever been inside one of these?" She asks.

He's trying not to show it but he is impressed. "Not something like this. My brother wanted to fly corporate."

"I heard about him... Logan, right?" She continues, "Didn't he also fly airshows?"

"A hard act to live up to," he answers.

"Is that what you're trying to do?"

For a moment there's an awkward silence. Then she turns and climbs the steps into the plane. He watches her body as he follows behind her.

They turn right as they enter the plane, first through a spotless galley. Fitted out in gleaming stainless steel and solid woods. Obviously designed to serve first-class meals, with a fully stocked wine refrigerator and drinks cabinet.

She leads him into the luxurious main cabin, "This is the cabin for our clients."

They take a moment to look around the immaculate and luxurious passenger compartment. It has handcrafted cream leather oversized seats, highly polished Walnut cabinetry with detailed inlays, and deep carpeting; not a mark on anything.

Laid out with separate areas for seating, entertainment and dining plus a stateroom at the rear. There is soft lighting and everything about this plane appears pristine, plush and perfect.

She turns back, and has to squeeze past him in the aisle; both apologizing to the other as they get close. She continues, "And up front. The area you'll be interested in."

Brooke moves forward and through into the cockpit and flight deck. Folding up the seat arm, she eases into the co-pilot's seat on the right. Following, Dave climbs into the left seat.

The cockpit is state-of-the-art magnificent, with a stunning array of controls, touch screen displays, instruments and switches; laid out in front of them and above their heads. Nothing like the archaic, scruffy panel of his crop-duster.

In the pilot seats they're close. Awkwardly they continue with the conversation.

"Come work for us. You won't start in this, but..."

She has the Gulfstream key ring in her hand. She takes off the keys and hands him the logo key ring. "Here, this is a start, you have the..."

As he reaches for the key ring the hangar lights go out.

The lights are controlled by a timer on the wall. It clicks to 8.00 PM, switching the lights off.

The hangar darkens almost completely.

In the cockpit it's hard to see one another. "The timer has switched off for the night," she says.

"I'll turn on the..." He looks over the instrument panel in the dim light, finds and turns on the aircraft-electrics master switch.

The panel comes alive, gyros hum, and screens and instruments light up. Warning lights for the engines, fuel, electrics, and hydraulic systems come on and pulse.

Dave and Brooke are bathed in the slow pulsing red lights.

An awkward pause. Then they both make to get up and bump heads.

"Sorry..."

"No, it was me," he says. "Sorry."

His hand reaches out to her forehead where he bumped her, they're close.

"I think we should…" She starts to say, then…

His hand moves from her forehead into her hair. Slowly he leans forward.

Her eyes close, leans toward him. Their lips touch. She catches her breath, a pause, and then closer again. They kiss. Then kiss again.

Both are breathing a little hard. But, after a moment she says, "We have to stop. Not here."

Just one word from him, "Here."

"No."

He kisses her again.

There's a long pause, then quiet and breathy she speaks again, "Here."

She removes her jacket. The instrument lights reflect red off her bare shoulders and arms.

It's almost dark around them.

She moves over to him in the captain's seat. Sitting on him, facing each other, they make love.

Her hair and tanned skin glow red from the slow pulsing lights and instruments.

CHAPTER EIGHTEEN

CONSEQUENCES

In the large hangar it's still dark and time has passed.

The side-door opens and Samantha enters. She calls out softly, "Dave. Hello? They said you were in here. Hello?"

It's dark but she sees the pulsing red glow in the Gulfstream cockpit. "Where are the lights?"

She turns, and it takes a moment or so for her to find the hangar light controls. She turns on the switches and the lights come brightly on, and she makes for the jet.

"Dave, you in there?"

She hears a footstep at the top of the plane's stairway. And Brooke exits the aircraft adjusting her jacket as she comes down the steps. A little embarrassed she smiles at Sam.

A moment and Dave follows a few steps behind her.

Sam holds him back as Brooke continues to the hangar door. Shaking her head she says, "You didn't...?"

Dave doesn't answer and continues after Brooke.

Sam looks up at the front of the Gulfstream, then after them as they leave the hangar.

She's pissed and, standing there with her hands on her hips she continues, under her breath, "That's not why they call it a cockpit."

Outside the hangar, Dave and Brooke walk back to the Jeep, laughing, enjoying each other.

They stop and kiss, his hands in her hair.

A car drives up and stops, it has a large badge on the door; Hodgeman the FAA district manager gets out. He approaches and stretches his neck. "Two hours ago a trucker, on a highway near Parker, was bumped by a crop-duster. It was identified by its 'N' number as the plane you were flying today."

He's taking his time. "You know the rules, unless over an airfield or crop dusting, no flying below 500 feet."

There's a pause. Neither Dave nor Brooke speak, not sure what to say.

He continues, "I promised you one more screw up and I'd have your ticket. This was it. You're grounded!"

Dave tries not to react as Hodgeman gets into his car and leaves.

CHAPTER NINETEEN

PLANS CHANGE

It's the next day at the crop-duster hanger. One of the mechanics works on a Pawnee engine. Reaching deep behind the mags to tighten a bolt, his wrench slips off the nut. He hits his knuckles on the firewall and swears softly.

In the background, Dave and Samantha stand by the aerobatic plane. They're disagreeing about something.

Dave shakes his head, "No."

Sam replies, "If it's to be paid off, one of us has to do it."

"It's too dangerous."

She faces him. "Oh sure, it's dangerous so you the man can do it, but I can't? That's bullshit."

"That's not the reason." This isn't what he wants.

"Then why? I fly as well as you do."

He shakes his head, not sure how to answer.

She continues, "You do know that you're not the only one living in someone's shadow."

He doesn't have an answer for this either.

She changes the subject. "Even if you put in an appeal to the FAA and it works, it'll take time." Sam says, "We'll miss this weekend at Chandler. The only other airshow this season is at Glendale. And you won't go there. Will you?"

Again he doesn't reply.

"Then it's settled. I do the Quad-cut."

CHAPTER TWENTY

CHANDLER AIRFIELD

It's two days later. The Chandler Airfield is packed with people, all here for an airshow. The sun shines in a blue sky dotted with white clouds, it's a beautiful day.

In the foreground close to the main runways are bright-colored show planes. Behind them stands the control tower with the field name in big letters on the front.

At show-line center the aircraft stand ready for the airshow performances. The next act is to be Samantha, she's sitting in the aerobatic aircraft.

Dave, kneeling on top of the wing is giving her last-minute instructions for the show. "On the third cut you make a complete roll, and then you're ready for the last ribbon."

He leans over and pulls her harness straps

tight. "Don't yaw, don't over-rotate."

The airfield is packed with a noisy, excited crowd, ready for the next act.

He continues, "You can't be down there out of altitude, speed, and ideas all at the same time."

But Sam isn't paying attention, she's busy signing an autograph for two drab young men. She leans out and gives back the book as she answers Dave, "Got it, got it, stop worrying. It makes me wish I'd listened to my dad when I was young."

"Why, what'd he say?"

"Don't know." She replies, "I never listened."

They both smile awkwardly at the old joke.

Dave jumps down from the wing as Sam closes the canopy and starts the engine. He moves back and stands next to Brooke, looking worried, who has come to join him.

"Does Wally know?" She asks.

Dave doesn't speak. She briefly shakes her head, she knows the answer.

Sam taxies away, waving to the crowd. As

she gets to the runway, she pushes in full throttle and roars down the strip.

Into the air and the maneuvers start immediately, a series of rolls. Then a loop, perfectly round.

Dave watches, his face showing concern. Easy to see this is not what he wanted.

It's a safe, precise routine, not Dave's angry, explosive flying. She doesn't fly as close to the ground nor stay near it for as long. As Sam gets into her routine, Dave relaxes. It's going well.

Sam tumbles the plane, then again. And again.

More maneuvers, some loops, a spin, and then she gets set for the main stunt. Four sets of ribbons come up, spaced a couple of hundred yards apart in show-centre.

The announcer, over loudspeakers, tells the crowd of the day's big event. His voice booms, "The Quadruple-cut... attempted many times, never done. Four ribbons to cut with wingtips and tail. Firstly the pilot, upside down and only feet from the ground rolls to cut the first ribbon with the left wingtip. Then rolls right to cut the second with the right wingtip."

The crowd is silent, on their feet, everyone watches as Sam barrels in toward the ribbons.

The announcer continues, "From there it gets harder and the pilot has to roll 270 degrees to cut the third with the tail. Then, while her head is spinning the most, she has to roll a full 360 degrees the other way to again cut the final ribbon with the tail. All this while just a few feet from the ground."

The wind catches the bright colored strips, they flutter harmlessly in the breeze. But the crowd are silent now, they know how hard this is. They know that nobody has completed this stunt successfully.

Sam dives and gathers speed.

She rolls the plane upside down, her head and the aircraft tail close to the runway. Easing the throttle back a little to control the speed, the plane approaches the first ribbon, Sam rolls over to the left wing and cuts it cleanly.

She rolls the plane to the right, 180 degrees, wing-tip just feet from the ground and cuts the second. It's going well.

For the third ribbon she has to make a difficult maneuver to roll the plane through 270 degrees the wingtip just a foot or so from the ground. But as Sam rolls towards inverted she lets the nose drop, the stick is not quite forward enough, it's just slight but the plane loses height. Barely a foot or so, but it's enough.

Dave sees it immediately. Speaks to himself, "You're too low!"

Fully upside down now the aircraft dips lower and the tip of the tail and rudder brush the ground.

Just a brush, a puff of dust. Nothing much.

But immediately it all goes wrong. As the tail touches there's a scream of shredding glassfiber and carbon. The tail is dragged along the runway. It pulls at the plane and slows it.

Sam pushes harder on the throttle, and the engine roars as she tries to get the aircraft away from the ground and into the air. But it's not enough.

At the show-line the crowd and Dave react. There is a collective gasp from the crowd, everyone's eyes on the plane.

IN THE AIR

Back in the plane, Sam pushes hard on the controls but the plane is not coming up. The tail and elevators control the aircraft's attitude, with the tip touching it cannot get the aircraft away from the runway. It needs power, a lot of power, to get it off the ground.

She has it at full throttle but nothing is happening, it's not enough, the ground still slows the plane and pulls her back.

It only lasts a second or so but feels like an eternity as the tail is dragged along.

Then the rudder is wrenched backwards and the aerodynamic balance gets ripped off. The top hinge explodes apart as the rudder is pulled to the rear. The top of the tail is also torn away, the empennage is a mess.

But this releases the plane and it comes off the ground.

As the crippled plane comes up Sam starts a roll to get it upright. However it rolls slow and slewed as the damaged rudder and tail are not enough to control the yaw.

The plane comes slowly up and around.

She has the control stick to the side to roll it, both hands to hold it over, and it's slowly coming upright. With her foot hard on the pedal, she has the damaged rudder jammed full over trying to stop it from yawing. Desperately trying to level the damaged plane and get it right side up.

Twenty feet above the runway, going fast, and almost under control. Almost.

ON THE GROUND

On the ground, Dave whispers, "Put it down. Just put it down. You can do this."

His fists clenched, willing the plane to fly.

IN THE AIR

She's now upright, the plane slewing sideways from the drag of the damaged rudder and tail, but still flying. She talks to herself, giving herself confidence, "Get it down. Put it down."

Sam eases back on the throttle, she's not flying quite as fast, and this helps to dampen the yaw. She's heading for a clear space between the runway and the crowd.

Maybe, just maybe she can do this.

The damaged rudder streams back in the wind. It hangs backwards at an angle, held by the cables and a single bolt at the bottom. This works for the moment but then the bolt-mounting shears off and the rudder tears backwards. But still held, trailing, by the rudder cables.

Barely a moment passes then the rudder is ripped away, the cables tear at the empennage and the rest of the tail comes away with them. Now there's no chance. Less than twenty feet in the air, the plane slews from the torque of the propeller, a wing stalls and drops, it hits the ground and it's all over.

The nose comes down and the aircraft, now slewing sideways, hits the ground churning up great lumps of earth.

One moment it's an aircraft flying, the next it's a ball of fiberglass and metal cartwheeling over the ground.

The left-wing shreds completely, and the right tears off. The main gear is torn away. What's left of the tailplane and elevators are ripped to pieces.

The aircraft kicks up and then tumbles

across the ground two more times. Buckled and torn it grinds to a halt.

The crowd surge forward, most held back by show staff. Dave fights his way through. He runs to the plane.

He gets to it just as the fire truck and emergency crews get there.

He tears at the wreckage but is pulled back by firemen. They pry at the cracked and broken canopy.

Sam can be seen, her face covered in blood, her eyes closed.

AT THE CROWDLINE

Hodgeman, the FAA manager, stands at the rear of the crowd line. His face shows no expression. He shakes his head, turns on his heel, and leaves.

He walks past two drab young men, busy looking at an autograph book.

Both look pleased with their day's bonus.

CHAPTER TWENTY-ONE

ACTIONS HAVE CONSEQUENCES

Dave's Jeep drives slowly on the road back to the crop-duster field. Inside, Dave is not paying attention to the other traffic, his face angry.

He hits the wheel, then again and again. Punches the windshield with his fist.

He jams his foot down on the accelerator, driving faster, his speed increasing. Serves from side to side, then overtakes on a corner, not caring if hit by oncoming traffic.

Arriving at the airport, he turns in still going fast, the Jeep's tires squealing. Arriving near the hangar he brakes hard and skids to a stop. Sits in the Jeep, hands still on the wheel, staring ahead.

One of the mechanics sees him slide to a

stop in a cloud of dust. He approaches. "You okay?"

No answer from Dave, then, "Where's Wally?"

The mechanic nods toward the hangar's side door. Dave exits and makes his way in. The mechanic follows.

Inside, Wally is working on the brakes of one of the Pawnees. Dave approaches and says something to Wally. The mechanic can't hear him but can see the reaction.

The older man stands, pushes past Dave and makes for the door. Dave goes to follow but the older man speaks over his shoulder, "Get away from me!"

Dave continues to follow but Wally stops and spins on his heel. It looks like he is going to hit the young man, but controls himself, and then speaks again, angry as hell, "Keep the Fuck away!"

The older man turns again and makes his way out.

Dave doesn't move, watches him go.

Then exits the hangar, gets back into his Jeep, and at speed he drives off.

CHAPTER TWENTY-TWO

SURE, RUN AWAY

Dave arrives at the Executive Airways building, slams on his brakes, skidding to a stop, ignores the lines, and parks. Exits the Jeep and enters the building.

Stepping out of the elevator he strides straight into Brooke's office. The receptionist does not try to stop him.

IN BROOKE'S OFFICE

Brooke has been crying, the handkerchief still in her hand. She looks up as Dave enters, before she can speak he says, "I'm leaving. There's nothing to keep me here."

She thinks this over, then, "Sure. Run away. Is that what you did last time?" She's angry, venting, and continues, "What about your stunt?"

He shakes his head.

"You might do it. Or kill yourself trying." She says. "But that would suit you too, wouldn't it?"

No answer.

The door opens and John Norman enters. Before either of them can speak he says, "Serve him the papers."

A brief pause then Brooke takes a legal docket from her desk, unhappy, but thrusts it at Dave. Then turns her back on him.

Norman addresses Dave directly, "There's a copy there for your boss. It was his plane, his company employed you, he is equally culpable for the damage to our aircraft." And waits for a response.

Getting none he exits.

Dave looks the papers over, takes a moment then he too leaves, slamming the door behind him.

Brooke stands by the window, looking out. A minute later, Dave exits the building and gets into his Jeep.

She watches him leave, her forehead against the cold glass. And, almost silently says, "Sure, run away."

CHAPTER TWENTY-THREE

SEDONA, AZ.

A buzzard, its wings spread, soars above a desert road. A thermal, an updraft of hot desert air, carries the bird high with no effort; it doesn't need to move its wings. It can climb thousands of feet and stay aloft for up to six hours while it searches for prey.

Below, Dave drives, his Jeep getting progressively dirtier. He travels into the wilderness, to the area of Sedona, Arizona.

Seen all around are desert mountains and red rock buttes, with high sheer cliffs and steep canyon walls, stark and remote.

The road worsens till eventually he's driving on a desert track. It ends at the edge of a deep canyon, he stops the Jeep. He exits and walks to the edge. Stands looking over the vertical drop, he disturbs rocks that fall. They drop thousands of feet, bouncing off the canyon walls.

Anger shows on his face, he looks down. It would be so easy to end it all here.

Above him a lone hawk circles, its head pivoting, glassy eyes watching below.

After a few minutes Dave turns, sits on the ground against the Jeep and looks out over a canyon. His face is still angry.

Time passes.

BACK AT BROOKE'S OFFICE.

Brooke works at her desk. She has files piled around her, she's working to forget recent events.

IT'S LATER AT THE CANYON RIM

Dave hasn't moved.

The only movement overhead. Hawks, buzzards, and other soaring desert birds.

He zips up his flying jacket, then reaches into the pocket and takes out the Gulfstream key ring. He looks at it for a moment then throws it over the cliff edge.

AT BROOKE'S OFFICE

Still working at her desk Brooke looks out the window, she takes a moment to watch the planes as they take off and land. She was not a pilot, she was more interested in the business of aviation, and had chosen not to follow that side of aviation.

She had been brought up in a small town close to Brew City, Milwaukee, in the mid-west. She had done well at school and obtained good grades, not good enough to get her into the top tier of universities, plus her parents would not have been able to afford it. But, her father, an engineer, who worked for Harley Davidson, and her mother, a primary school teacher, had been proud of her when she graduated from high school with a high GPA, more than enough to get her into the University of Milwaukee.

She knew what career path she wanted to follow. Her parents would take her, when younger, along with her brothers to Wittman Regional Airport for the annual Oshkosh airshow and fly-in convention.

Just an hour's drive from their house they would spend days, each year, walking around the many aircraft exhibits and displays, watching the airshows and meeting with other aircraft enthusiasts.

Her brothers and father would spend most of their time in the military aircraft display areas or around the small private planes, but she was more interested in the passenger-carrying aircraft; particularly corporate jets. She would visit the display areas of Bombardier, the Canadian private jet maker, the French company Dassault, and the American maker, Gulfstream; plus other smaller private plane makers. For a while she thought she might work for one of these companies but eventually decided she wished to work with the end users, the customers who bought and operated the planes and those who travelled in them.

After graduating with good grades in Computer Sciences from Milwaukee she enrolled at The University of Chicago, Booth School of Business. Two years later she had her MBA, a Masters in Business Administration; specializing in Business Analytics.

It was at this time, on a weekend with

her brothers, she was introduced to one of their friends who also shared their interest in aircraft. They had a brief affair before he left to join the Army to fly attack helicopters. They had tried to stay in the relationship but found it almost impossible when he was going through his training years and she was finishing her MBA with the intention of moving west, so they had parted.

She met him again four years later. He had taken early retirement, or at least this was what he told her, it had seemed vague as to why he had left; but regardless he had left the Army and was employed ferrying aircraft around the world. He was delivering a small Cessna jet to her company and had taken her to dinner that evening.

Before she knew it she was back having a relationship with him. He had returned to live in the mid-west but travelled extensively, always seeming to be able to pass through Phoenix on his way somewhere. He would be delivering aircraft or be on his way to a remote location to pick up a plane and would drop in for a couple of days or so.

His life seemed adventurous, moving planes all over North America and often between countries, however, not always legally. Sometimes he would be chased out of a country while trying to collect a plane, he would laugh as he explained how he just managed to stay ahead of the authorities.

He also told the story of flying an ex-military plane out of Prestwick, Scotland. He had been told he had the wrong paperwork and was instructed to return to London to resubmit the correct papers to leave British airspace. He took off, with clearance only to fly south, but had turned west, towards his final destination, America. By the time anyone had noticed he was on the wrong course he was out of British airspace; and had ignored their radio calls. He laughed as he explained he fed the paperwork, out of the cockpit window, page by page to the waters of the North Atlantic.

When questioned why he didn't fly for an airline or as a corporate pilot, he would shake his head and give a vague answer about not being tied to one place.

Then, for no apparent reason, she heard no more from him. Checking with her brothers they also had lost touch with him, the last they heard he was again ferrying planes across the North Atlantic. She tried contacting the company he had worked for but they couldn't, or wouldn't, help; he had, apparently, collected a plane in bad weather and, when last heard from, was believed to be flying to Iceland. The circumstances seemed vague plus she could not pin down exactly where or when he had last been heard from.

Brooke looked out the window at the planes, taking off and landing, coming and going. It was two years since she had last heard from him. Against her structured and controlled life he had cut a dashing figure and lived in an excitement-filled world. She had enjoyed her time with him, no question she had been in love, but had known that it would end, however perhaps not like this. Hopefully, he was still out there, but she knew he would not, one day, fly back into her world; and even if he did she knew she would not, could not, accept him back.

She shook her head, turned and returned to her desk and her work. Grateful that, for a moment, her mind had been off the subject of Dave and Sam and what had happened.

AT THE CANYON RIM - IT'S LATER

The sun sets over the red peaks as darkness falls. The birds no longer fly.

Dave sits, not moving, his back against a Jeep wheel.

Still staring out over the canyon, his mind in turmoil, but now he's thinking of what happened at Glendale fourteen years earlier.

He remembered that the authorities didn't know what to do with him after the accident and subsequent events. There had been some talk of criminal proceedings or some action to punish those involved. Wally and the FAA manager, Hodgeman, were questioned by police and the National Transportation Safety Board.

But nothing came of it, it was like the officials could not agree who had caused what had happened or who should be held responsible. He found out much later that charges were considered but after much disagreement, they had been dropped.

The only thing that those in authority could agree on was that Dave should go to a foster home or an institute of child care. They had tried to contact relatives for him, but no one knew if he had any.

After a couple of weeks he was asked if he wished to be placed with a family who would take him into their home. He refused this and any other offer they had, so was sent to live at an institution for homeless children. He didn't mix with the other kids here, they tried to befriend him but he neither spoke, listened nor joined them in any activity. Eventually, the other teens shunned him, but after a while they started taunting him and he got into fights with the other boys. He soon learned how to stand his ground and win, sending other kids back, bloodied when they tried to challenge him.

After a couple of months Dave knew he couldn't stay; didn't know why he just knew he wanted to get away. So one morning he slipped out; it was easy as during the day there was no security or locks to pen them in. He hitched his way to the Greyhound station. He had just a few dollars but it was enough to buy a one-way ticket to Denver.

There was no good reason to go there, he'd just picked a place, and had enough money for the ticket. He didn't know anyone and didn't have a place to stay so Dave lived on the streets. For a couple of months he survived, he stayed away from drugs but still got into trouble.

A couple of gang members cornered him and tried to take his leather jacket; probably to sell. He'd fought them and, determined he would not lose his brother's jacket, he beat one of them senseless, putting him into hospital; the other ran away.

He was picked up by the Denver police the next day. Even though he was defending himself and was stopping them from stealing his jacket, charges of assault were made.

He was 16 now and was put into the juvenile court system. There they tried to find out his history and background; where he was from, if he had family or a criminal record. He told them nothing other than his first name and gave a false surname.

He was brought in front of a judge and a deal was struck between a public defender, on behalf of Dave, and the court. Give the authorities his true identity, allow them to check his record and if there were no outstanding warrants he would be released. His answer was no, he'd take the incarceration figuring they would have to release him eventually.

A couple of months later, in juvenile

detention, he had a run-in with two imprisoned members of the same gang as the kid he'd put into the hospital. They came for him at night but he stood his ground and fought back.

Again he was approached by the authorities who offered him the same deal, give them his true identity and he could be released. Once more he refused.

The gang members came for him again, but once more he stood up and fought; this was not going to stop.

Back in Arizona, Wally had been trying to find him and had sent out missing-child notices, photos, and information packages; even a small reward had been offered for his location. Wally received a tip on Dave's whereabouts and contacted Denver juvenile services.

Wally gave them the boy's history but when Dave was told he could be released into Wally's custody, he refused, he didn't want to go back to Arizona. A couple of weeks later, Wally and Sam came to Denver. He then again, to everyone's frustration, said no to the offer of living with them.

Dave had stood in the visitor's room and watched as Wally walked back to his car. He could see Sam, whom he'd only met a couple of times before, sitting in the passenger seat. He saw her get animated when Wally, he figured, explained to her that Dave was not going to accept the offer of a home.

He then watched as Sam, who was about 14 at the time, get out of the car, slam the door and stride toward the building; a determined look on her face.

Two minutes later she was escorted into the room. She stood in front of him and said, simply, "You need a family and I need a big brother." She paused, "Pack your things, get in the car, you're coming with us."

And strode out.

He was left to think about it but did not move from his seat for over an hour. During that time Sam and Wally waited in the car, he watched them from the window. They didn't speak to each other and they never moved.

After another half hour, he got up and asked to be taken to the prison food hall. There he approached the two gang members he'd been having trouble with.

Although still not 17, and smaller than the

larger of the two, he said, "If you think there's still a problem between us when you get out, I'll be in Phoenix, Arizona. You come look me up, I'll be waiting."

He then informed the prison administration he'd changed his mind. They gave him back his things, including his brother's jacket and he was released. He threw his stuff in the back of the car and got into the rear seat; he didn't speak, but it didn't matter as they never said a word either. Wally started the car and in total silence they drove back to Arizona.

The two gang members never came looking for him, he never saw them again.

When they got back to Phoenix nothing was said, by Wally or Sam, about the previous year; he was simply accepted into their home. He was given his own room and told he would do chores and, at weekends and during school breaks, he and Sam would help with the spraying operation. They would mix the chemicals, fuel and load the dusters, hold wrenches for the mechanics, and generally help around the airfield.

Just over a year later, after Dave had received his High School Diploma, Wally put him into the Chandler-Gilbert Community College Part 147 Airframe and Powerplant Mechanic program, more commonly known as A&P school. He attended two years of community college and at the age of 20 he received his license to repair and maintain aircraft.

Dave showed no interest in learning to fly, however. When Sam started lessons he had also been asked but said no. Wally didn't question him on it, figuring Dave had his own set of demons regarding flying after what had happened to his brother.

What made a difference however was Sam when she started her pilot ground-school studies. To prepare for her private pilot license, she asked Dave to help and to quiz her on the questions and answers. They spent hours going over mock exams together preparing her for the difficult written test. When Sam passed, he then helped her prepare for the oral exam, a rigorous hour or so of verbal questions and prep for cross-country flying. Then, finally, after she took her flight test her first passenger was him.

This would be his first time flying since his brother had flown him under the bridge on the way to Glendale. When she first asked him, he said no. This continued for a week till one day Sam, who was now 17, stood in front of him and simply stated, "Dave, get in the damn plane. We're going flying."

For a moment he stood there, stoic. But she wouldn't back down, she stayed in front of him, her hands on her hips, refusing to move. It took a long minute then he nodded his head and got into the passenger seat, hooking up the single lap strap, and they flew.

He remembered that Wally had watched while Sam took him for that flight, he didn't comment or say anything; just a nod of the head when they returned. Dave had sat alone for an hour or so near the J-3, deep in his own thoughts. Neither Wally nor Sam had disturbed him. She told him after, they figured it was better that whatever problems he still had he should handle them on his own. If he had wanted help this time, they reckoned, he would ask. After an hour he made a decision and asked if Wally would, after all, teach him to fly.

Wally simply nodded and said, "We start tomorrow."

The tables were then reversed as Sam now helped him through ground-school, quizzing

Dave constantly till he felt confident to sit his exams and do the oral test.

After he completed his private pilot's flight test both he and Sam, who was now 18, studied together for their commercial pilot's license. It was taken as natural that both would continue on to fly dusters and help Wally with the business.

He had not discussed it with either Wally or Sam but he considered the two things that helped him get through his problems were, first, learning to fly. It gave him purpose and a future. And second, it would be Sam, who had looked to Dave to be a big brother, and in her he had found family again.

BROOKE'S OFFICE

Brooke stands at the window, looking out at the dark. It's late, there are only a few flight operations at this time of night, so there is little movement at the airport.

There is, however, a full moon in a clear sky; it lights up the mountains that surrounded Phoenix. The barren rock and sand backdrop looks almost surreal in this light.

HOSPITAL

It's after midnight at the St. Joseph's University Hospital in Phoenix.

The surgery ward had been busy that day and it had gone into the evening but had now slowed. Only a few people and nursing staff remained in the wing. It's dark outside, still a few more hours or so before the sun rises.

Sitting in a waiting room is Wally, his face blank.

BROOKE'S OFFICE

More files are on Brooke's desk. It's dark outside but she still works. The building is empty other than for her.

BACK AT THE HOSPITAL

It's early morning, the sun has started to rise.

Wally hasn't moved, it's obvious he's been here a while.

He is approached by a doctor, who wears scrubs and looks tired, he has worked through the night.

His face set, showing no emotion, Wally stands.

The doctor nods and says, "You can go in now."

CHAPTER TWENTY-FOUR

RETURN

On a desert road, coming down from the mountains, Dave drives his Jeep back to civilization.

It's later the same day and his Jeep drives into the car park for the Hospital.

Dave makes his way in, asks for directions at reception and is pointed to an elevator. Exiting, he makes his way along a ward corridor, checking the number as he enters a room.

Samantha sits in a hospital bed. Her broken leg elevated. The side of her face is still raw. Even bandaged, strapped up and hurt, this girl is attractive.

With her stands a young man in scrubs.

She sees Dave and smiles, "Oh, sure. Finally, you come to see me."

"I needed to get my head together." He smiles, "A couple of days."

Sam replies, "Nearly a week."

An awkward pause. Then she continues, "I'm being well looked after. This is my doctor."

The young man smiles, "An intern actually."

A moment passes then Dave says, "I came to apologize."

"For what?" She replies, "It's a broken leg and a few cuts and bruises."

The young man in scrubs speaks again, "It's a bit more than that."

"Right. But I'll heal," she says.

The intern nods.

A moment as Dave looks at both, a questioning look on his face.

"I'm sorry. Where are my manners?" She says with a smile. "Dave, this is Harry Clems." Introducing him, "He's been looking after me."

Dave smiles.

Then Sam changes the subject, "The worst thing, I trashed the plane."

"We'll build another," replies Dave.

She nods but then turns serious. "First. Go see Wally."

CHAPTER TWENTY-FIVE

MOVE FORWARD

Dave's Jeep pulls up outside the hangar.

Inside, Wally works on one of the Pawnees, changing a rudder cable. Dave enters and approaches the plane. If Wally notices he doesn't look up.

Dave waits a moment then speaks, "I'm sorry."

No answer. Wally continues with his work. There's a long pause, and then the older man answers, "She could have died."

Dave nods.

There's another long pause. Then Dave answers him, "You know that I would have—"

Wally breaks in before he can finish, motioning, "Pass me those cutters."

Dave gets them for him. He tries to continue, "I'm sorry, You know I would...."

Again he's cut off by the older man, "I know."

There's an awkward pause.

The older man then continues, "They served me the papers." He pauses, thinking about something. He shrugs his shoulders. "Time for me to sell up, pay them, and retire. Spend some time doing something else."

"I'll do the Quad-cut." Answers the young man.

"No."

"I can do it." Dave answers.

Wally replies, "I said, no."

"I'll use the Stearman. My brother flew one in airshows, so can I."

A pause as the older man goes over it in his mind, then, "It doesn't have the guts. The engine's lightweight."

Dave answers, "We use the Pratt & Whitney off the wrecked duster. It's big enough. You rebuilt my brother's plane, do this one."

"I also rebuilt his…". The older man shakes his head.

"We can do this," states Dave.

Wally takes another pause for thought. He looks to the yellow Stearman at the rear of the hangar. Near to it, still up on jacks, stands the big damaged Ag Cat.

The older man walks over to the Stearman, trailed by Dave. But stops and shakes his head. "No. This is bullshit, I can hang an engine on it but the stunt will kill you."

"I can do it. Logan could—"

"He had a patience you don't have. You fly like you're mad at the whole damn world."

No answer. There's a long pause.

"You taught my brother, teach me."

This is still not what Wally wants. He shakes his head once more.

Dave continues, "You lose everything if I don't fly it."

Wally doesn't answer, but he's thinking about it. Gives it some thought, he doesn't want to do it. But —

After a moment the older man continues, "The only airshow possible is this coming weekend. If we're going do it we start now."

Dave nods.

Looking at the Stearman and then over at the other plane, Wally continues, "With that big engine she'll be mean. Give her a chance and she'll bite you."

Dave pauses, thinking about it, but has the final word, "She won't bite me."

CHAPTER TWENTY-SIX

A BIGGER ENGINE

Removing the Ag Cat's propeller they chain the big radial engine to a shop crane. Dave unbolts it from the frame as Wally welds up a new engine mount.

They wheel the massive engine to the Stearman. Removing the plane's smaller motor in turn.

Wally patiently explains a point to him, sketching out what they have to accomplish. Dave nods, and the two work closely together.

The work isn't easy, wrenches slip in the confined engine space and knuckles bleed.

Working close, the strain shows on both faces.

Outside it's getting darker. They work through the night, not stopping. It's dawn and they continue into the next day.

Time passes as they attach the mounts, the engine, pressure pumps, inlet manifolds, exhaust, throttle, mixture, choke and propeller control cables. Fuel lines, oil lines, oil returns, oil breather, and electrical connections.

Then they mount the propeller. It's massive, three-bladed and black in color.

It's dark outside, they work into the second night without sleep.

They both look weary. Wally asks, "I'm hungry. You?"

With a nod from Dave as he continues to work, Wally phones in an order.

Time passes. A car arrives outside and they hear a knock at the side door. Wally points for Dave to get it.

Dave goes to the door, and waiting outside is a Domino's delivery girl, a college kid, maybe 19 or 20, holding a pizza box.

She smiles brightly, "You ordered a pizza?"

This stops him, he looks at her vehicle, a beat-up older car with a DOMINO PIZZA sign on the top.

The girl waits for an answer. Wally works on the engine, he looks over at Dave. Seeing the effect this has on him.

She taps her foot, waiting, "Buddy? Your pizza?"

He answers, "Yeah. Sorry."

He fumbles into his wallet for a tip then takes the box. He carries it back into the hangar, looking at Wally, who looks up.

"What?" Says the older man.

"Nothing."

Dave sits at the desk and takes out a slice, Wally sits on an old couch next to it and reaches into the pizza box. Neither saying a word.

They eat, and then it's back to work. Into the second night without sleep.

It's past midnight and Dave drags himself off to sit on the couch and eat a cold piece of pizza. He falls asleep, the last slice still in his hand, untouched.

Wally comes over and takes away the pizza slice, eases him fully onto the couch, and puts Dave's flying jacket over him.

He goes back and works through the second night to complete the plane. Occasionally looking up at the sleeping young man.

CHAPTER TWENTY-SEVEN

IT'S A NEW DAY

It's early the next morning, the sun comes up.

Inside the hangar, Wally shakes Dave. "Wake up, kid. We're done."

Dave gets up from the old sofa, he shakes his head to clear the cobwebs. Runs his hand through his hair.

The older man opens the hangar door. "Let's go. Time to have some fun."

HALF HOUR LATER

We hear Dave's voice over the radio, *"Wally, I'm not having fun."*

Wally is in one of the Pawnees, flying, looking down at the airfield.

Below him is Dave in the Stearman, skidding and swerving down the runway. Weaving from side to side as he tries to get the big-engined beast under control and off the ground.

Wally presses his joystick radio button to talk to him, *"Go easy on the throttle and be careful with the rudder, it's not balanced for the big motor."*

Below him, Dave takes another giant swerve across the runway.

"I said, be careful with the rudder." From the older man.

Finally, the plane comes off the ground and into the air. The swerving slows as Dave gains more control.

"Follow me," orders Wally.

Both planes climb, Wally on a steady course. Dave, still weaving but climbing fast to catch him up.

The older man continues, *"How'd she feel?"*

Dave, in the cockpit of the Stearman, answers, *"Good, lots of power."*

"*Okay.*" Says Wally, "*Let's find out what this bad girl will do.*"

He leads him through a series of maneuvers, loops and rolls, getting Dave used to the plane. The young man follows close behind.

They roll left, right, a loop, Dave tumbles the plane. Then again.

After a few maneuvers Wally asks again, "*How's she doing?*"

"*Rigging's off, she yawing left and is nose heavy. Need to adjust it when we get down,*" answers the young man. "*But for the moment I can handle it.*"

Wally peels over, diving down, speed increasing, followed by Dave. Down to the surface of a wide river.

A bridge comes up, Wally flies beneath it. Dave rolls upside down and goes under inverted. The upside-down wheels almost brushing the underneath of the bridge.

Wally soars upwards. "*Stay down there, stay inverted. Get lower.*"

Dave continues to fly upside down. Low to the water. Flying with his tail a few feet from the surface.

The river widens to a lake.

"Lower still." From Wally over the radio.

In the cockpit, Dave's concentration is complete, right-hand clenched tight on the joystick.

At this speed the water rushes by. Upside down, the plane's tail is close to the water, with his head in the open cockpit just above the dark surface. The sound of the large engine reflects back up, loud, scary.

"Damn! This low enough?" Says Dave.

"You're doing good, kid. Now, let's calm you down."

"Calm! Here?" From Dave.

The older man patiently explains, *"We don't need you angry. Something goes wrong, we need you calm and cool."* His voice in Dave's headset. *"Adjust the trim and relax your hand."*

Dave, with his left hand, pushes the trim lever gently forward. Feels the weight come off the joystick. His right hand relaxes on the stick. The water rushes by, the noise deafening, but he's doing as he's told.

Wally speaks again, *"Now, hold the stick with just your thumb and two fingers."*

"No!"

Wally's voice is calm and reassuring. *"Do it kid, I won't let you come to any harm."*

A pause as Dave takes this in, then relaxes his fist from the stick and gently uncurls his fingers. Holding the stick with just his thump and a couple of fingers.

Still flying just above the surface.

"This time, just a finger and thumb, and relax."

Amidst the screaming noise, Dave relaxes his hand and flies with just his thumb and one finger on the control stick. His left hand again adjusts the trim, allowing him to hold the plane in position with just the gentlest of pressure.

Upside down, just a foot or so above the water. He's calm.

Dave, his voice quiet, *"I have it. I can feel it."*

His hand gentle on the stick.

Wally speaks again, *"Good. Now, if there's a problem and the tail touches I need to know the engine will pull you back up."*

"What?"

"I strengthened the tail. Put it on the water."

"What?" From the young man. *"No!"*

"Do it. If you want to do the Quad-cut, you need this. Get the tail on the water."

A long pause then Dave eases the stick back, bringing the plane lower. The tail skims the surface.

Dave grits his teeth, and holds it there. But then relaxes. The tail touches, skips, and once more it skips, then comes down and stays.

The upside-down plane speeds across the surface, the tip of its tail on the water's surface.

The water claws at it, but he increases power. On the aircraft panel the altimeter dips to the bottom of the zero mark.

The engine screams as it pulls the aircraft along, the water trying to drag it down.

Wally speaks again, but this time just to himself, "You can do this…. Stay calm, kid."

In the cockpit Dave stays calm, his hand gentle on the stick, Mr Cool.

On the lake, near a creek in a small boat, two older gentlemen sit quietly fishing. Their eyes are near closed as they sit half-asleep in the warm sun.

The water calmly laps against the side of the boat as they spend their peaceful day.

Then, abruptly, there's a roar of a powerful engine and a large bi-plane tears past in front of them, the noise tremendous. Upside down, the tip of its tail dragging in the water.

Close behind, going like a bat out of hell, a crop-duster chases after it.

Neither man stops fishing. Only their head and eyes move, in unison, as they track the inverted plane as it speeds past.

For a long moment neither speaks.

Finally one of them comments, "That has to be hard on your skivvies."

The second man, open-mouthed, just nods.

It's later, side by side, Dave and Wally head for home. Both are quiet, lost in their thoughts.

They come over the fence and land.

CHAPTER TWENTY-EIGHT

PERMISSION?

THAT EVENING

It's after sundown, ablaze with lighting the Sky Harbor International Airport lights up the sky and the surrounding land.

Overseeing all aircraft operations are the Air Traffic Control and the Terminal Radar Approach Control (TRACON). Both are housed in the control tower that stands 320 feet high and provides air traffic controllers with unobstructed views of the entire airfield and its surroundings.

Seen from the large plate windows of the control tower, passenger jets take off and land from the three runways. Multiple aircraft, large and small, line up on taxiways.

Looking out at the busy airfield Wally and the FAA manager are in the middle of a conversation.

"Young men live and they will die, there's nothing we can do about it. You can try and stop them, make rules, tell them what they can and can't do. But, in the end they will..." Wally pauses and looks out over the airport.

Then turns back, explaining, "Jim, he's not trying to kill himself, he needs to do this. There's something inside him, driving him. It's not just the money." Again he pauses. "If Logan was here, he'd do it... but he's not. This boy has got to be given his chance. And that is up to you."

Hodgeman stares out at the jets coming and going, his only movement is to stretch his neck.

In the background, controllers are busy directing aircraft. We hear from a speaker, *"Phoenix Tower, this is Trans World Four Twenty-Two Heavy. With you at Beeline Yankee, descending through seven thousand."*

The controller replies, *"Roger, Trans World*

Heavy, proceed on a heading of one nine zero, report a six-mile D.M.E."

Not speaking, Hodgeman continues staring out at the busy airport.

CHAPTER TWENTY-NINE

PAINT

THE NEXT DAY

Back in the hangar, Dave and Wally work on the Stearman. Dave is busy unbolting and pulling off the spray gear and Wally works on the tail.

"What'd he say?" Asks Dave.

"He was still thinking about it when I left."

"Doesn't matter anyway. The only airshow for months is tomorrow at Glendale."

Wally doesn't reply, just nods.

For a moment Dave doesn't speak, but then, "You know I can't go there."

No answer.

"I can't."

Silence, neither speaks. Outside the sun is setting.

EVEN LATER

It's getting darker outside the hangar now. Face mask in hand Wally prepares a paint gun. Behind him the Stearman stands sanded, taped-up and masked, ready for painting.

He nods to the hangar door. "Get out of here while I paint." A pause and then he continues, "I want it done for tomorrow."

Dave doesn't say a word, his face clouded in thought, but he makes for the door. Wally puts on the face mask and begins spraying.

As he paints, the Stearman's faded yellow color changes to deep red, the color of Logan's plane.

Dave walks out into the night, he pulls on his flying jacket, it's getting cool out here. He stares off over the runway into the desert darkness. Behind him, from the open hangar door, he can hear the air-compressor run as Wally paints.

CHAPTER THIRTY

BACK TO GLENDALE

As Dave looks out to the desert the noise of the air-compressor seems to blend into the sound of an aircraft engine.

His mind goes back to Glendale, many years earlier, when he watched his brother in his Stearman taxi past toward the runway.

FOURTEEN YEARS EARLIER

Logan taxies the plane to the run-up area. He looks down into the cockpit and quickly checks his instruments, oil temp and pressure okay, electrics, both mags and fuel cock are turned on, and he tugs his safety harness tight.

He swings the plane around to line up on

the runway. Pushes the throttle fully forward and the engine roars, the aircraft quickly gains speed, the tail comes off the ground and a few seconds later the plane takes off.

BACK ON THE RAMP

Standing in front of the crowd Hodgeman, the FAA agent, notices some drops of oil left behind; below where the aircraft had stood. Just a couple of drops, nothing much.

He walks over to it and wipes a finger through the oil smear. Looks up to Wally who glances down at it.

Wally shrugs. "Radial engines go through oil like water. I'd be more worried if it didn't leak."

"I'll call him back." In his hand, Hodgeman has a hand-held radio.

Wally shrugs again. "Up to you."

Hodgeman takes a moment, he's thinking about it, he knows that old radial engines are known for leaking. Particularly when they stand and the engine cools, oil seeps past the piston rings and valves of the lower cylinders, and into the exhaust.

He shakes his head, doesn't call, and continues to watch.

IN THE AIR

Logan blasts past the crowd and does a couple of loops then a roll. In the cockpit the hand of Mr Cool is gentle on the stick.

The sun shines off the bright red paint, and at the show-line the crowd are "oohing... and ahhing," as he goes through his routine.

But below the plane some oil trickles backwards along the belly skin and into the slipstream. It slowly grows in volume.

Logan flies a series of loops and rolls.

It's beautiful up here, a lovely Spring day, blue sky, puffy white clouds.

He does a hammerhead, then a spin, and another loop.

The act builds to a finale and some show-staff come out to the runway and pick up two long poles.

Strung out between the poles is the ribbon for the 'ribbon-cut' maneuver.

Logan lines up on it, the middle sags to about fifteen feet above the runway.

The ribbon flutters in the breeze.

The plane dives. The noise increases as the young pilot shoves the throttle fully forward, the big engine screaming.

Enjoying himself, Logan has just a couple of fingers on the stick, relaxed.

But below, on the aircraft's belly, black oil streams back. It's gotten worse. A lot worse.

On the cockpit panel the oil pressure gauge drops unnoticed into the red as he concentrates on the ribbon. The plane is too far away for anyone in the crowd to see the escaping fluid.

Pointed downward the plane accelerates, the airframe shaking from the excessive speed. The noise from the big radial engine is tremendous.

Still calm and enjoying himself he rolls the plane upside down and flies less than twenty feet above the ground. Logan is aiming to cut the ribbon with the tail.

He drops even lower. The tail is now just above the runway.

Faster, closer. The ground speeds by, close to Logan's head in the open cockpit. The noise is overpowering as the runway tarmac reflects the sound of the engine back up.

As he approaches the ribbon, however, he sees the oil. As now, with the plane inverted, it's running down the fuselage sides in thick steams and is blown by the slipstream towards him.

His eyes narrow.

Before he can do anything the engine makes a distinct crack. Once. Twice. Then there are sickening, grinding noises as the oil-starved engine shreds metal.

A piston rod is punched through a cylinder wall as the crankshaft comes apart. The timing gear gets torn out of sync and the engine stops producing power. The propeller now acts as an air brake.

Logan's hand tightens on the stick. He pushes it to gain height. But there's no power in the crippled engine to pull the plane away from the ground.

Shuddering and upside down, the

Stearman slowly sinks down to the runway.

The upside-down tail touches first. Sparks fly and there's a scream as metal shreds.

The tail drags on the runway, slowing the plane.

His left hand rams the throttle back and forth, trying to bring the engine alive and pull him off the ground.

But it's futile, the plane slows.

The top wing touches and the upside-down aircraft slams down, ripping open the fuel tank in the upper wing. Avgas pours out over the runway and plane.

And over Logan in the open cockpit.

The Stearman skids under the ribbon. Metal buckles and bends. The tail drags, and sparks fly.

A trail of fuel streams out behind it.

Sparks from the dragging tail ignite the highly flammable Avgas. Flames trail for hundreds of feet.

The upside-down Stearman, ahead of the flames, slides to a stop.

The top wing keeps the plane from coming down completely on Logan. He's alive. Hanging in his straps.

He shakes his head, trying to clear it and wipe the fuel out of his eyes. He looks back and sees the flames racing toward him.

Tears at his harness. Hanging upside down he fights the release. It opens, he drops and hauls himself out of the cockpit and starts to get clear.

A firetruck heads for the plane, its siren wailing.

It's a race between the flames and the fire engine. The firetruck goes as fast as it can.

The flames win and the plane and Logan are engulfed in fire.

The horrified crowd watch in silence as the fire engine skids to a stop. Within seconds it covers everything in foam.

The crowd run forward, the FAA inspector looks at the oil spots on the ground then he also runs.

Past a teenager.

A young boy wearing his brother's leather

jacket, staring at the burning plane.

A tear runs down the boy's face and falls onto the jacket.

Then he starts to run. Slowly at first then picks up speed.

Screaming his brother's name.

BACK TO TODAY

Dave still faces the runway and looks out into the night. Slowly he shakes his head and turns back to the hangar.

CHAPTER THIRTY-ONE

THE MAIN EVENT

It's the next day at the Glendale airfield.

The airfield has changed little in fourteen years. Hangars, parked planes, taxi-ways, runways. The control tower sits back from the runways, with the name, GLENDALE, in big letters on the front.

Once again there is a crowd and the excitement of an airshow.

But this time it's jam-packed with people, the word has gotten around, that there's to be an attempt at the deadly Quadruple-cut.

At the front stands the red plane, and with it are Dave and Wally. The mechanics are busy checking it over, one has the cowling up.

He calls over, "It needs some oil."

Dave looks to Wally, who nods, "It's okay." And motions to the mechanic to put some in.

Refueling the aircraft, the second mechanic has a large hose in the upper wing, filling it to capacity.

Dave has started to pace up and down, his face set but determined. It's clear he doesn't want to be there. But...

Through the crowd the FAA manager approaches. He ducks under the tape and makes for them. Dave joins Wally and they stand together, waiting. Around them it goes quiet.

Hodgeman addresses Wally, "I'm not letting Mr Sanders fly."

Dave starts to speak but is stopped by Wally.

The FAA manager continues, "He doesn't have an airshow performer's card."

"It was confiscated after the incident with the truck," states Wally.

"Correct," answers Hodgeman. "As per FAA regulations, a pilot is to have his performer's card on him when flying his act."

There's a pause as if the FAA man is

expecting an answer from Wally.

Not sure what to say, Wally hesitates for a moment, then he continues. "But if he had a card, a new card?" He asks, "He'd be able to fly?"

No answer.

"I can write him that card," Wally states, tentatively.

"As per the rules, an examiner has to have seen the performer do his act within the preceding seven days." Hodgeman is quoting from the regulations.

Wally answers, "I'm a qualified examiner and I've seen him perform within the last couple of days."

It's as if Hodgeman has been waiting for this and replies, "This wouldn't have anything to do with a pair of planes flying under a bridge and scaring some fishermen on Lake Havasu the day before yesterday? In direct violation of the '500 foot' rule?"

Around them everyone holds their breath. Wally is not sure how to answer this.

Nobody speaks or moves...

... silence.

Brooke, who has been standing unnoticed with the crowd at the tape line, steps forward.

Dressed in jeans and a light shirt, she answers in a clear and firm voice, "I think you'll find that was a couple of my pilots."

All eyes turn to Brooke. No one is expecting her to be here.

"Your pilots?" Hodgeman is stopped for a moment by this.

She doesn't waver. "They're preparing to do an airshow act at the weekends."

Nobody moves.

"And, I believe," she continues. "They were practicing at the lake two days ago."

Now Hodgeman is not sure what to say, he asks, "To do an act...?"

No answer, she just holds his gaze. After a long moment, she continues, "I'm pretty sure I can get them here to confirm it."

Hodgeman tentatively answers, "I'm not sure I..."

"Or I can make a phone call," she says.

He doesn't believe her for a minute but...

There's a long pause, and then Hodgeman shakes his head. "Give him his ticket."

He looks to them for any comeback. Nothing. People around them are still holding their breath.

Nobody moves.

He speaks again, "I said, to give him his damn ticket!" And turns to leave.

Realization sets in, and the mechanics grin their big toothy grins as Wally searches for a pen and paper to write out a performer's card. "Give me a piece of paper, somebody, anything."

The FAA official takes a step to leave but is stopped by Dave. The young man says, "Thank you."

It appears Hodgeman has something more to say, he's thinking something over, but settles for, "I should have stopped your brother that day."

Dave answers, "But you didn't know what would happen."

Hodgeman answers, "Then I should have stopped you, after."

He's not talking about the accident, it's

something else, back then.

Dave answers, "You couldn't have."

Hodgeman thinks about it for a moment, but remains silent, then turns and leaves.

Dave watches him go. Then approaches Brooke. He stands before her. "I'm sorry... the other day, in your office."

For a moment she doesn't answer, thinking something over. She makes up her mind and answers, "A while back I was engaged to one of our pilots."

He waits.

"We were close to getting married. I was ready. But he wasn't, hadn't grown up. Playing with aircraft, a hot-shot." She pauses. "Eventually he moved away. I heard he was killed. Flying. It was just a matter of when and where."

Brooke takes a second, then goes on, "It's the same with you, isn't it? It's just a matter of when and where."

She waits for him to deny it. He doesn't.

"Go, fly." She states. "Go do your stunt."

He asks, "You'll be here when I get back?"

She takes a moment then shakes her head.

He thinks for a moment but then reluctantly accepts her answer and nods.

He walks away making for his plane, takes his leather jacket out of the cockpit, and goes to put it on.

"You don't need it, kid."

Dave turns to the older man.

Wally continues, "I know it's your brother's jacket and you think you should wear it for him. But it's time to let go of the past and some of the anger it has caused. I don't think your brother would have wanted you to be as unhappy as you've been."

Dave gives it some thought and passes it over to Wally. The older man continues, "We'll talk about it again sometime. But for now... go fly."

Dave nods and turns back to the plane.

Two drab young men duck under the tape and quickly make their way to him, an autograph book outstretched. He looks at them and the book and shakes his head. "No, afterwards."

They are led back by show staff.

The first young man says, "He's not going to do it. Hasn't got the touch." Loud enough for others to hear.

The second speaks out, equally loud, "He'll be in the dirt!"

Dave ignores them and climbs onto the lower wing of Stearman and steps into the cockpit. He straps in and starts the engine.

Brooke comes and stands next to Wally. And asks him, "Will he be okay?"

Wally doesn't answer.

The plane starts to move, turns, and Dave taxies away, fast.

As he leaves Brooke faces Wally. "All right, I want to know. Tell me what happened. Here at Glendale."

"His brother crashed."

"That much I've figured out. There's more, tell me."

It's obvious Wally doesn't want to explain.

She continues, firmly, "Tell me."

After a pause, he answers, "The engine I rebuilt... the crankcase cracked and blew the oil. It seized."

She waits, there's more. And Wally tells her what happened

GLENDALE, 14 YEARS EARLIER

An ambulance races away from the airport.

A gurney is rushed from the ambulance into a hospital. Dave, in tears, goes with it.

Wally continues to explain, "Logan was badly burned. Beyond recognition. Got him to the hospital. He was on life support. Dave never left him, wouldn't leave him."

In an Intensive Care Unit room, Dave sits by a hospital bed.

It's hard to see with the dressings and tubes, but it's obvious that his brother is badly burned.

Wally continues, "Logan was never really conscious, he'd breathed in the flames, was never going to recover, he was going to be a vegetable."

A doctor looks at the young boy, but there's nothing he can say.

"After two weeks he slipped into a coma." The older man's voice low. "Hodgeman and I went to the hospital."

Brooke queries him, "The FAA man?"

"He had flown with me and Logan's father in Nam, known Logan since he was a kid. Gave him his first performer's ticket. Thought he should have stopped him when he saw the oil on the ground."

The younger Hodgeman and Wally draw screens around the bed.

As they stand by the door, Dave, crying, kisses his brother's forehead and starts pulling tubes. Finally pulling a plug from a wall socket.

Alarms start and pounding is heard from outside the door.

"While we stopped anybody coming in."

The heart-rate monitor goes flat-line and a shrill monotone alarm sounds.

Dave stands, stolid, by his brother's side. Tears stream down his face.

Brooke is stunned. "You let a kid…? He was fifteen years old."

No answer.

It's hard to go on, but she continues. "He'd lost his parents two years earlier. Then this… his brother?"

Still nothing from the older man.

Brooke goes on, "And now we're back here, again, at Glendale? Damn you, Wally. Damn all of you!"

Absolute anger on her face. She could so easily hit this man.

"Whatever happens today, this ends here. You understand, this is the end of it."

No answer.

She repeats herself, firmer, "Do you understand?"

He nods.

AT THE RUNWAY

Dave turns the aircraft, stops, and quickly runs through his pre-flight checks.

Over the loudspeaker system the announcer tells the crowd that there will be an attempt on the Quadruple-cut, and his voice booms. "The Quad-cut has kept the airshow world abuzz with excitement, this deadly stunt has been tried numerous times. The attempt today will be made by one of the country's best new pilots. The younger brother of famed Logan Sanders, who, I'm sure you will remember, flew his last airshow here at Glendale many years ago."

Dave revs up the engine, and the sound echoes around the airport.

AT THE AIRFIELD CARPARK

Hodgeman, the FAA manager unlocks his car door.

Hears the roar of Dave's plane. It stops him. He stretches his neck. A pause then he makes a decision and turns.

Face set, he makes his way back to the flight-line.

BACK ON THE RUNWAY

Engine roaring and show-smoke on, Dave takes off. He immediately snap-rolls the plane close to the ground.

Rolls left then right. The plane spinning around. He starts his routine as he intends to end it, fast and only feet above the runway.

If any of the crowd were seated, they are standing now.

IN THE AIR

In the cockpit the world spins violently around Dave.

His teeth are bare as he fights the G forces from the intense maneuvers.

On the panel, the altimeter needle climbs then falls to zero then back up.

Dave roars along the crowd line and tumbles his plane, end over end, across the sky.

ON THE GROUND

The crowd are on their feet. This is what they're here for, the main event.

Joining Brooke and Wally is the FAA manager. Wally turns, notices him and nods. A thin smile is all he gets as a reply.

IN THE AIR

Dave tumbles the plane.

Then again. End over end.

The furious, out-of-control maneuver far too close to the ground.

His flying is aggressive, harsh, and violent.

The plane claws its way higher. Climbing vertically in the sky, show smoke pouring out behind.

Dave chops the power and his plane hangs in the air. Then falls over onto its back and down, through the smoke, toward the ground. Falling backwards, into an inverted spin, getting lower.

At the last moment Dave slams the power on, kicking the rudder hard over, the spin stops and the plane rolls upright, engine roaring.

Then he tears along the crowd line and tumbles the plane again, the plane cartwheeling. Tumbling over and over. Far too low.

Then slows, gains height, and Dave prepares himself.

IN THE COCKPIT

Through clenched teeth, Dave speaks into his boom mic. *"I'm ready. Get them to raise the ribbons."*

His hand is tight on the stick, he flexes his fingers, but then goes back to gripping the stick tight.

ON THE GROUND

Four sets of ribbons come up, spaced a couple of hundred yards apart, held by a pair of helpers for each pole.

IN THE AIR

Dave dives the plane, the engine screams as he slams the throttle forward.

Hurtles downhill, accelerating, the ground

coming up.

Closing fast.

ON THE GROUND

At the flight-line Wally quietly speaks to himself, "Cool it down, kid. Cool it down."

IN THE AIR

Unconsciously Dave has tightened his hand on the stick, he's tensed up. Nearing the ribbons he grips the joy-stick hard. His knuckles are white.

Just feet from the first ribbon he knows something isn't right. He speaks to himself, looking around. "It's wrong, it's wrong."

For a moment he pauses, he's almost on the ribbons, but he knows something's wrong.

The young pilot makes a decision and heaves the stick over and jams on opposite rudder. This skids the plane sideways, kicking it to the side, missing the pole and ground by inches.

The Stearman zooms up and turns away, as

if the pilot intends to leave.

ON THE GROUND

A collective gasp comes from the crowd, and two drab young men enjoy the moment.

"What did I tell you, he can't do it, he'll be in the dirt." Says the first, smirking.

The second nods in agreement. "A smoking hole in the ground."

TO ONE SIDE

Brooke, who has been standing with Wally, shakes her head and says quietly to herself, "It's just a matter of when and where."

She turns, and unnoticed walks away from the flight line.

AT THE FLIGHT-LINE

Wally pulls his handheld radio from his belt. Speaks into it, *"Calm down..."*

IN THE COCKPIT

Dave shakes his head, trying to clear it.

Hears Wally, over his headset. *"... no more flying angry."*

Listening still he turns the plane, brings it around and sets up again.

"You do this calm, Dave, cool." But Wally gets no answer. *"You understand? Stay cool."*

A moment then Dave visibly relaxes. Presses the talk switch on the joystick. *"You want cool, Wally?"*

Down the hill he goes, the engine screaming.

He uncurls his fist, relaxing on the stick, holding it with just a couple of fingers and thumb. With a small smile on his face, he transmits again, *"Cool we can do... it's time to Limbo."*

ON THE GROUND

"What? No. NO!" Wally states, trying to stop him.

But from the radio, *"Sorry, Wally. Got to."*

The older man rolls his eyes and the mechanics grin. Hodgeman looks away as if he didn't hear it.

Behind them a few people, who have heard the radio, laugh and chant. "Limbo... Limbo."

Picked up by more of the crowd. And the mechanics, in front, wave their arms encouraging them. Then more people start.

Till everyone is screaming. "LIMBO... LIMBO. LIMBO... LIMBO."

IN THE AIR

Dave roars down, his hand relaxed on the stick.

He rolls inverted and, upside down, limbo's under the first ribbon.

His upside-down wheels just clear the tape, the tail just inches from the ground.

Then pulls up, rolls 360 degrees around to the left, then down and limbos under the second.

Then up again to roll 360 degrees to the right, spinning the plane over, then down to limbo under the third and fourth. Then pulling up and away.

An amazing series of rolls and maneuvers between and under the ribbons.

ON THE GROUND

The pole holders grin as the plane, at their level, flashes past them.

At the flight-line Wally and the mechanics laugh. Hodgeman, with a small smile on his face, shakes his head.

And the crowd scream their approval.

IN THE AIR

Dave gains height and turns the aircraft back towards the ribbons. And says over the radio, "Okay, this time."

Rolls the aircraft out of its turn, dives, and picks up speed. This time he's going to do it.

The noise is almost unbearable. The aircraft tears down towards the ribbons, down towards the ground, and down into the belly of the beast.

Dave's hand relaxes on the stick, he holds it with just a thumb and two fingers. Mr Cool.

Rolls the plane upside-down. Close to the ground.

Just feet from the first ribbon he rolls 270 degrees to the left and cuts it with his left wing tip.

The crowd roar, on their feet, necks craning to see.

Less than a second from the first cut he rolls 180 degrees to the right and cuts the second ribbon with the right wing tip.

Then rolls back 360 degrees, a complete turn just inches from the ground to cut the next ribbon with the right wing tip again.

The crowd screaming.

Next, it is the hardest part, he has but moments to complete the last and most dangerous maneuver. He rolls left 450 degrees, an amazing turn from right-wing tip over to right wing tip again, then another turn to end upside down, his tail scant feet from the ground.

Even though his head is spinning he steadies the upside-down plane. Reaching for the ribbon with his tail.

But the last ribbon has drooped to within feet of the ground.

ON THE GROUND

Wally notices. Speaks quietly to himself, "The ribbon's sagged."

IN THE AIRCRAFT

Dave sees that he has to get lower.

Upside down, teeth clenched, he eases back on the stick. Doing the same thing that Sam did on her attempt, trying to get down.

Dave thumbs the radio switch on the joystick, and calmly transmits, *"Tail's going to hit."*

IN THE AIR

The upside-down plane comes down even lower.

The tail touches the ground. Skips.

Then touches again and drags. Sparks fly.

The tip bends and shreds. We've seen this before when his brother's plane was dragged down.

Metal grinds, and screams.

Dave pushes the throttle forward. The engine starts to pick up, but stutters.

The tail still scapes on the ground, the noise unbearable.

Under his breath Wally speaks to himself again, "Stay calm."

In the cockpit, Dave, upside-down, is calm, and relaxed, his hand gentle on the stick.

But the tail still drags. The inverted plane rockets along, in the open cockpit Dave's head is just inches from the ground.

Sparks flying.

The engine hiccups. Hiccups again.

ON THE GROUND

Wally clenches his fists and grits his teeth. Nobody notices, all eyes are on the plane.

IN THE AIR

It's as if time stands still. The world is in slow motion, as the crowd waits for this plane to either come off the ground or sink down to it. The tail still dragging.

Then the engine thunders. And roars. Comes up to full power.

The black propeller hauls the plane back into the air and off the runway.

Just in time for the last ribbon.

The tail slashes through it. The fourth and final ribbon.

All four ribbons flutter down.

The crowd go crazy. Cheering. Screaming.

Dave soars up and does a victory roll.

The mechanics jump and whoop. Wally turns and shakes Hodgeman's hand.

In the background the announcer tells the crowd they've just seen the first Quadruple-cut ever performed and that the pilot will receive a sponsored prize of a million dollars.

Skidding through the sky and landing quickly, Dave puts it on the ground and taxis fast to the flight-line. He spins the plane around.

Stops.

He kills the engine, the propeller stops, and the engine noise is replaced by the crowd screaming.

A grinning Dave is pulled from the cockpit by the mechanics.

The crowd, unheeding the show staff, rush forward.

An autograph book is knocked from the hands of a drab young man. Kicked and stood on, the pages scatter and are trampled underfoot.

Mobbed by the smiling happy crowd, Dave looks for Brooke. He can't see her.

Calls to Wally, "Where is she?"

Wally shakes his head, he can't hear over the noise.

Dave searches...

... twists and turns, looking...

... between people he sees her, tears in her eyes, she wears his leather jacket.

He pushes his way through the crowd. Stands before her. "That job. You still offering medical and a pension?"

For a moment she doesn't answer. Then smiles and replies, "And all the pizza you can eat."

Both laugh and try to kiss but are mobbed by smiling kids wanting autographs.

As Wally, Hodgeman, and even the mechanics are being asked for their signatures.

WE PULL BACK AND SEE FROM ABOVE

The mechanics examine the Stearman's damaged tail and a smiling FAA manager shakes hands with Wally again.

At the flight-line a girl in a wheelchair arrives, pushed by a young man we last saw in a hospital room. Both look around at the excitement, not quite sure what's happened.

And in the middle of a mob of people a young pilot kisses a girl who wears an old leather flying jacket.

CHAPTER THIRTY-TWO

FLY FURTHER AWAY

That was the last time Dave flew in front of the crowd. He never stepped foot in an aerobatic plane again.

Brooke, however, continues with Executive Airways, she's now the vice-president of marketing, for the entire company, but still operates from Phoenix. The company still flies the original Gulfstream 700, plus they have bought three more.

She also has her Honda Civic still but drives it only occasionally, it sits parked next to a BMW, a larger SUV model; she needs a bigger car these days. Enough room for her, two children and their father, Dave; who still insists on driving.

She keeps the Honda and has made a

mental note that when their children graduate from high school, and they have grades high enough to get them into Arizona State University, she will buy them Civics. And she will help them pay their way through college.

AS WE MOVE FURTHER AWAY FROM THE AIRFIELD AND RUNWAYS

Sam went on to make a full recovery. She still flies, in fact she now runs the crop dusting business, and it's doing well. She married her doctor and they now have two children, both girls. She's promised them that as soon as they are tall enough to reach the rudder pedals and see out of their grandfather's Piper J3, she will teach them to fly.

Wally retired but still comes to the airfield to work on planes a couple of days a week. He's still as bad-tempered and grouchy, except when he's with his grandchildren.

Dave still flies, but now he pilots Gulfstream 700's, out of Phoenix International, from the left seat as Captain for Executive Airways.

And every now and then, when he flies over the Glendale airfield, he thinks back to those days. He looks down and sees the runways, the tower, and the planes parked there.

As he flies on he looks a little further away, a couple of miles or so from the field, to where sunlight reflects off water.

There he sees a large metal double-arched framework, made of steel and concrete, that spans a river. A river that's lined with wildflowers, trees, and red rock cliffs.

Where, a long time ago in another lifetime, two brothers in a Stearman flew under a bridge on their way to an airshow.

The End.

From the author:

I hope you enjoyed *An Airshow to Die For*, as much as I did writing it. If you did, please leave a positive review for the book, it would be greatly appreciated.

You are welcome to contact me with any comments, my email is rroth1000@gmail.com

The following are the first few pages of my recent book *Death of a President's Son*. I hope you enjoy them.

PROLOGUE

ATLANTIC OCEAN. JULY 16, 9:41 P.M.

Eight miles out from Philpin Beach, off Martha's Vineyard, water quietly lapped in the gentle swell. Hardly a breeze stirred in the hot summer evening.

At the ocean surface the visibility was poor, a dark haze obscured distant waves. Inland weather stations had forecast an almost clear evening, expecting four to eight miles of visibility. But here, devoid of any feature, the horizon faded and blurred into the haze.

However, the scream of an over-revving aircraft engine was easily heard as a small plane spiraled down out of control.

In the poor visibility it was difficult to tell the plane's color or markings, but it was easy to see it was too late to do anything. At two hundred miles an hour it crashed into the water's surface. The force sheared the engine from its mounts and the wings tore from the plane's fuselage.

Waves rippled out as the water swallowed the broken aircraft. Within a minute, however, even the ripples were gone. With nothing left on the surface to show what had happened and the ocean returned to its silence.

SATURDAY, JULY 17

The next day dawned clear in upstate New York, many miles from the sea. By mid-morning the sun had risen in a clear beautiful sky over a small private airfield.

A four-seat blue and white Cessna 182 sped down its single runway. The plane was twenty-plus years old, its paint lightly faded, but it still climbed strongly into the air. A bird dodged the high-winged aircraft and raced to the trees that lined the small strip.

"You got it?" asked Billy Hill, sat in the plane's left seat in jeans and a blue work-shirt, his hands folded in his lap. "Or is it flying itself?"

To the right his fourteen year old daughter, Penny, strained to see over the aircraft's nose. "I have it," she said, her right hand on the control column, her left on the throttle and both feet on the rudder pedals. "Or maybe it has me. I swear this thing has a mind of its own."

"Not if you keep on top of it."

"What is it with you and planes? Sheesh, old people."

"Hey, enough of the old if you don't mind." He slackened off his seat belt a notch. *Did all teenagers think anyone near forty was ready for the old people's home?*

"I don't get it, I spend time with you and it's planes and flying," said the girl. "With mom it's boats. She's booked us on a cruise in a couple of weeks. Give me a break, a cruise, next it'll be all-you-can-eat buffets and wearing polyester."

Billy scanned the instrument panel, ensuring everything showed in the green and then gazed out of the side window to the countryside below. He took in the lakes, trees and wildflowers that spread out to the horizon in the hot July sun. Not yet midday the temperature had already climbed into the eighties and heat-waves shimmied off the ground.

"It gives you cancer," she said, casually.

One eyebrow raised, he glanced at his daughter. Her short dark hair spiked up over lively brown eyes. Tall for her age, probably from her mother's side, she had been able to reach the rudder pedals for the last year.

Reluctantly he asked the girl, "What?"

"Wearing polyester," she grinned. "It gives you cancer."

He turned back ignoring her.

Her flying had improved over the past two weeks she had spent vacationing with him at the cabin. He felt comfortable letting her handle takeoffs and landings now. For two of his twelve years with the military he had been a flight-instructor and knew when somebody could fly or was just going through the motions.

A muted ring brought him back to the present and he quickly scanned the panel instruments. It was not coming from the aircraft. Other than a stall-warning his mid-eighties Cessna had little in the way of audible alarms.

He pulled his cell phone from his pocket and, pushing his headset back, put it to his ear.

A muffled, "Billy?"

To cut the engine noise he stuck a hand over his other ear. It quieted enough that he could recognize the voice of his boss, Jim Anderson. Billy did not know him particularly well. Jim was in charge of the office in Washington, D.C., and seldom seen out of the building, whereas Billy worked mostly in the field. So far, however, he had been a decent enough man to work with.

"Yep. We're flying, but I can talk, I'm a passenger." Billy looked at his daughter. "More of a hostage really."

Stomping on the right rudder pedal and jamming the control column to the right Penny rolled the plane hard over. The left wing came up to a steep angle as she pulled the aircraft around.

He didn't react, Billy was used to his daughter's flying.

"I've been trying to reach you," his boss said.

"Had the phone turned off, in case the wicked-witch called."

"Don't call Mom a witch," Penny said, rolling

the plane level, then steeply back the other way to the heading. Both of them hung, weightless, in their seatbelts as the Cessna flew into a pocket of air and dropped.

Jim's voice sounded tense. "A light plane went down last night."

"Who was in it?"

His boss ignored the question. "How far are you from Essex County airport?"

"New Jersey?" Billy asked.

"Unless you know of any other Essex County. You need to be there, now."

Anderson sounded testy and in Billy's seven years working aircraft accidents it was unusual having his questions ignored.

"Who am I working with?" Billy asked.

There was a long pause from the other end.

"Who, Boss?"

"Steve Bishop, Barbara Nicholls and…"

"No. Don't put me on with…"

"Get there now."

"I can't work with…" The phone went dead.

Billy shook his head, he didn't need this.

Penny glanced over. "Something's gone down?"

Billy didn't answer, his mind churning. He grabbed a flight-map from the door pocket and located the airport. After a rough calculation in his head for winds and distance he figured it would take two hours to get there. He checked the plane's fuel gauge, they had just filled the tanks, there was enough.

He pointed in the direction he wanted to go. "Kid, I got a problem. There's no time to get you home. You're coming."

"Not more flying," she said with a practiced grimace.

"Your mother will kill me. First chance I get, you're gone."

"Who have they put on it? That you can't work with?"

"Nobody."

He dialed a frequency into the VOR direction indicator and tossed the folded map up onto the dash. Then took the controls and swung the Cessna around fighter-plane steep. Matching the compass and VOR he leveled out and pointed the aircraft southeast.

Quietly, and with a shake of the head, Billy answered her question again. "Nobody."

ESSEX COUNTY AIRPORT, NEW JERSEY, TWO HOURS LATER.

"For a full stop, Four Four November," Billy told the tower.

"Make right downwind, cleared to land runway two eight. Four Four November." The radio answered.

"Right downwind, runway two eight." Billy repeated and turned the Cessna onto the downwind leg of the landing pattern, dropped the flaps and slowed. Onto base then final, descending, the aircraft came over the boundary fence and bounced onto the runway.

They turned onto the taxiway. "I think that's the terminal building." Stated Penny, pointing.

Billy nodded and headed the plane toward it. Taxiing the Cessna up to the tie-down area, he switched off the engine and the propeller windmilled to a stop.

Exiting the aircraft, he reached into the back for a large dark blue bag. Standard issue and nicknamed a 'go bag,' the lettering along the side read NATIONAL TRANSPORTATION SAFETY BOARD. It contained three days of clothing, a couple of manuals, a flashlight and a few small tools. Billy carried it constantly, either in the plane or thrown in the back of his Jeep. He unzipped it and pulled out an NTSB cap and name badge.

Hat on and pinning the badge to his shirt, Billy strode toward the pilot's area of the large terminal building. Penny grabbed her backpack off the backseat of the plane and hurried to catch up.

Billy took a step through the door and stopped, expecting it to be quiet. Normally a pilot's lounge is a place to relax and grab a quick coffee while a ramp-rat, a line-person, checked the oil and refueled your plane. Not today. Today government agency people crowded the place. FAA,

CAP and NTSB personnel, name caps and badges identifying them, milled about. Busy people setting up tables, computers and communication equipment forming organized units. The noise level high, the place was quickly being turned into a makeshift command center.

"All this for one small plane?" Billy said to no one.

He saw his group, wearing NTSB caps and jackets, standing around a desk in a corner. As he drew closer, he recognized the voice giving a briefing. It belonged to Barbara Nicholls, the team IIC, the Investigator-in-Charge.

She looked different from the last time he had seen her a couple of weeks earlier when she'd laid down some rules he didn't think necessary. He tensed up, but then just as quickly he relaxed. *Get it out of your mind, I can work with her.*

Paying closer attention, he noticed the

change in her appearance. She had cut her hair, the shorter brunette bob made her appear younger than her late thirties. Distinctly more business-like and that, he was sure, was what she was going for. Professional looking in a dark gray suit and crisp white blouse she talked in a firm, determined manner, everyone's attention fixed on her. No question who was boss.

Folding his arms, he stood at the back of the group and listened.

"I don't want any bullshit or excuses," Barbara said. "You people are to work together and with the agencies around you. At the moment it's still search-and-rescue and we're helping with that." She looked over and noticed him.

It stopped her for a moment and he saw her eyes flash anger. Then with a slight headshake she resumed the briefing. "But our primary role is the same as always, if this plane has gone down it's up to us to find out why. And make no mistake everyone is watching us on this one. Everyone. You have your assignments. Let's get to it."

She dismissed the group and came over to him. If she looked upset before, it had now raised up a notch.

"You're late. We started the clock six hours ago," Barbara said. Then noticed Penny. "What's she doing here?"

Penny smiled politely.

He ignored her question. "Why so many people?" Billy asked. "Who's gone down?"

"See Steve, you're working support for him. He'll bring you up to date."

"I'm working for *him*?" This was not something he wanted to hear.

Barbara stepped closer. "You have a problem with my decision?"

"He doesn't know his ass from a hole in the ground." Billy was not going to be intimidated by her.

"You weren't here, he was," she said. "I've

made the decision. Now get up to speed, you've wasted enough time." Without waiting for an answer, she turned to walk away. Then stopped and turned back to him.

"Just so you know," Barbara's voice lowered. "I didn't want you here, I still don't and given the chance I'll make sure you're gone first chance I get."

With that, she strode away.

Billy shook his head and watched her go. "God, I hate that woman."

For a moment there was silence, then Penny chimed in, "Yep," she said. "Ex-wives can be a bitch."

He gave his daughter a sharp look and considered chastising her for her choice of words, but let it go.

Penny reached up and kissed him on the cheek. "It was a great couple of weeks, Dad. Thanks." She hoisted up her backpack and grinned. "But I'd better go with the wicked-witch."

And follows after her mother.

The previous are the first few pages from my recent book, *Death of a President's Son.*

John F. Kennedy Jr.'s last flight told as a docu-drama, including the days leading up to that fateful night. We also follow the story through the eyes and actions of an NTSB go-team as they investigate how and why this plane crashed. Plus, we see the effect JFK Jr.'s personal life had on events. This book allows us to understand easily how things went so terribly wrong and why the son of a president died.

The following are reviews for this book:

***** It is a must to read. I could not put this book down.

***** This guy can write!

***** Great book, wow, this author is one in a million. Exciting book.

***** This is a great book.

***** Wonderful and well thought out by a renowned pilot.

***** Excellent read.

***** The author's experience and knowledge are really what made the book so fascinating. Great Read.

***** Amazing book.

You can find it in Kindle or paperback version on Amazon.

Printed in Great Britain
by Amazon

35351064R00142